Confession of a Tattooist

Tattoo Series, Volume 1

Lexy Timms

Published by Dark Shadow Publishing, 2016.

CONFESSION OF A TATTOOIST

First edition. February 12, 2016.

Copyright © 2016 Lexy Timms.

Written by Lexy Timms.

Also by Lexy Timms

Alpha Bad Boy Motorcycle Club Triology
Alpha Biker

Fortune Riders MC Series
Billionaire Ransom
Billionaire Misery

Hades' Spawn Motorcycle Club
One You Can't Forget
One That Got Away
One That Came Back
One You Never Leave

Heart of the Battle Series
Celtic Viking
Celtic Rune
Celtic Mann

Justice Series
Seeking Justice
Finding Justice

Managing the Bosses Series
The Boss
The Boss Too
Who's the Boss Now
Love the Boss
I Do the Boss
Gift for the Boss - Novella 3.5

Saving Forever
Saving Forever - Part 1
Saving Forever - Part 2
Saving Forever - Part 3
Saving Forever - Part 4
Saving Forever - Part 5
Saving Forever - Part 6
Saving Forever Part 7

Southern Romance Series
Little Love Affair
Siege of the Heart
Freedom Forever
Soldier's Fortune

Tattoo Series
Confession of a Tattooist

Tennessee Romance
Whisky Lullaby

The University of Gatica Series
The Recruiting Trip
Faster
Higher
Stronger

Undercover Series
Perfect For Me
Perfect For You

Unknown Identity Series
Unknown
Unpublished
Unexposed

Confession of a Tattooist
Tattooist Series #1
By Lexy Timms
Copyright 2016 Lexy Timms

Tattooist Series

Confession of a Tattooist
Book 1

Surrender the Tattooist
Book 2
Coming March 2016

Book 3
Coming April 2016

Find Lexy Timms:

Lexy Timms Newsletter:
http://eepurl.com/9i0vD
Lexy Timms Facebook Page:
https://www.facebook.com/SavingForever

Lexy Timms Website:
http://lexytimms.wix.com/savingforever

Description

Hawk Reynolds is the hottest tattooist in the city, and not just because he's a terrific artist and knows how to use the needles to turn skin into art. He's panty-melting hot thanks to his jet-black hair, tattoo sleeves, and a body that incites fantasies.

Plenty of women come to the shop just to let him put his skilled hands on their bodies, but none of them ever come close to touching his heart. Until the day a regular shows up with her bestie, Joy, in tow.

Joy's a shy and intelligent blonde who has no idea just how beautiful she is, and she's not really interested in getting a tattoo; but she *is* interested in the art she sees on the walls, and the bad-boy tattooist who drew it. Joy's been burned before by men who just wanted to date her because her father is billionaire Terry Reed. She's determined to never be used that way again, but as her steamy relationship with Hawk turns into something meaningful, she begins to wonder if she's the user.

Hawk tells her there's one thing he won't put up with: lying. And she's already lied about who she is.

CHAPTER 1

The tattoo shop was located right in the beating heart of Los Angeles. The storied nightclubs around it drew in rock stars and starlets, groupies and wannabes every single night, while the trendy eateries and the cheap souvenir shops were a major attraction to the busloads of tourists that were dropped off for a few hours to walk those star-lined streets.

The massive façade of Mann's Chinese Theatre, the street performers, and the bright blue sky all combined to create a carnival-like atmosphere, and more than one tourist had missed their original hop-on, hop-off bus and had to catch another because they got caught up in the sights and sounds of the busy spectacle.

More than a few of those tourists got back on the bus wearing fresh ink too, courtesy of the hottest tattoo shop in L.A., Hawk's Folly.

The shop was always packed, thanks to the artistic stylings of its artists and the reality show that had been filmed within it for a few seasons before Hawk, the owner, pulled the plug and said he wasn't willing to keep working with cameras in his face every single moment.

Hawk was one reason so many flocked to the door and beyond it to the well-lit studio with its funky leather couches and bright paintings. In a city filled with gorgeous men, Hawk stood out as one of the hottest.

He was tall, six-foot-two, and leanly muscled. His jet-black hair, cut into an elegantly messy style, and strong jaw blended and contrasted with his full lips and high cheekbones. He'd been offered modeling contracts and television parts over the years, but he always turned them down because he wasn't interested in fame.

The reality show was the only thing he'd agreed to, and he had agreed only because he'd just opened the shop and knew it needed the exposure if he was going to make it a success. He'd brought a full client list with him from the shops he'd worked at before, where he had honed his skills and learned all he could about how to run a shop and run it successfully, but he'd needed something more.

The show had been an irritant. He hated being on camera, and often closed his door to keep the cameras out, forcing the crew to focus on the rest of the tattoo artists and the customers instead. He'd hoped it would let people know he didn't much care to be bothered unless someone was interested in a tattoo, but instead it had gotten him tagged with rather idiotic monikers like 'mysterious and temperamental', which only sent more women to his door in droves.

Some came for tattoos, but most were there to try to catch a glimpse of the 'mysterious and temperamental' Hawk.

Refusing the show's new contract hadn't hurt business a bit. In fact, more people who actually wanted tattoos and not just the cache of having been on a television show came once the cameras were gone.

Business was booming.

As he pulled to the curb on his chromed-out custom bike, a smile lifted his lips as he took note of the people already pausing to look into the windows of the shop.

He swung off his bike easily and took a paper bag from the saddlebag. The bag was splotched with grease and sent out a heavenly aroma of roasted pork gently simmered in citrus and garlic. He carried it into the shop.

Haley, his piercer, looked up and said, "Damn it, Hawk! Really? Pork carnitas?"

He lifted a dark eyebrow. "What's wrong with carnitas?"

"Nothing," Hayley replied with a groan, "Except I'm on a diet."

Hawk gave her a stern glance. Hayley was five-foot-seven and weighed a scant hundred pounds. "Where, precisely, are you going to lose weight from? Your brain?"

She waved a hand at him. "I got tapped to do a spread in a magazine. I have to make sure I don't have a spare ounce of fat."

He sighed. He hated Hollywood's crazy beauty standards. Those standards expected women to be almost unbelievably, and unhealthily, thin. "What magazine?"

She named a well-known publication that used to specialize in nude centerfolds but now featured scantily-clad women because, in an age dominated by free Internet porn, the visuals of nearly-nude women were bigger sellers than totally naked women. "I see. Hayley, if you lose any more weight you're not even going to be able to lift a sandwich, much less eat one, and I'd highly suggest you eat one instead."

She giggled. "Are you saying I'm too thin?"

"Yes."

Her eyes lit up. "Wow. Thanks. Oh, I got that audition later today, so Barry's going to be in the piercing station after two. Cool?"

"Yeah, no problem. Sure you don't want a carnita?" He waved the bag in the air, letting the aroma of the food within waft toward her.

Hayley flashed forked fingers at him and said, "Get thee behind me, Satan."

He laughed. "More for me then."

All the tattoo stations were already filled. Each artist had their own room, and most of the doors stood partly open or tightly closed. He could hear the whirl of the guns and chatter, and smell fresh ink. That sound and fragrance always made him smile, and lightened his mood. He loved his shop. He paused long enough to straighten the edges of a few framed paintings before heading back to his office to eat his carnitas and go over a few things before he started his day.

He set the bag down on his desk, took off the heavy leather jacket, and slung it across the back of his chair then sat down. He pulled out the two delicious carnitas, the meat so slowly-roasted it was guaranteed to melt in his mouth. He bit deeply, relishing the fresh pops of lime, lemon, and cilantro, and the tangy bite of garlic.

Lunch finished, he sat back and checked his schedule. His mood immediately soured. He had a custom piece scheduled today, an extensive work that would take at least four hours.

He didn't mind the time or the work. He disliked the fact that the work had to be done for a spoiled young pop star who always thought he should get everything for free, and who'd once walked out without paying at all.

A discreet phone call to his manager had sent the money he was owed Hawk's way, but he was in no mood to deal with the little shit, and he was slightly angry that he had forgotten to tell the new receptionist and scheduler that the kid was persona non grata in his shop.

He'd remedy that today, except it was too late to cancel now.

His spirits lifted when he saw a note reading; 'Pix is coming in today after six.'

Pix, his nickname for Pixie, was a hell of a woman. She loved tattoos and punk rock music, kept her hair a bright but dark blue, wore clothes she salvaged from thrift stores and consignment shops, and rescued dogs from death rows and off the sides of freeways. Pixie wore a broken heart the size of Texas right on her sleeve, swore she'd never fall in love again, and wasn't interested in him at all, except as a friend. Over the years they had developed a sibling-like bond, and he always enjoyed seeing her.

They hadn't seen each other in a while. She'd saved up all her money to go off to the Philippines to battle against the illegal dog meat trade, and he'd wondered if she'd made it back.

It seemed she had.

Pix would most certainly take the bad taste of his client out of his mouth. Her ribald sense of humor was enough to make any day brighter, and he was really interested in finding out how her life had been since the last time they'd seen each other.

He stood and stretched and the headed toward the room where he worked. He might not like that rotten little asshole he had to work on today, but it was no excuse not to do a great job.

CHAPTER 2

"Come on, Joy, go to the tattoo shop with me."

Joy lifted an eyebrow and tried to repress the smile that wanted to lift her mouth. Pixie was impossible to resist under the worst of circumstances. These weren't the worst, but she had absolutely no intention of going to a tattoo shop with her. Pixie could talk people into anything, she'd seen it with her own eyes, and while she appreciated the colorful and lovely tattoos that Pixie had she didn't want any for herself.

Nope.

She didn't find the idea of willingly submitting to pain enticing, and, since she'd had more than enough pain in her life as it was, she had no interest in willingly allowing someone else to hurt her either.

Besides, getting a tattoo wasn't in her books. She couldn't. She could probably stand the pain but she might not live through the process, thanks to the blood thinners she was on.

Pixie cut into her thoughts, "I know you don't want a tattoo, but you could use a night out. And since you refuse to go to a club..."

"Clubs bore me," Joy put in.

"Okay, and since you refuse to go to see a band with me or anything else that's cool, I totally insist you go with me to the tattoo shop."

Joy waffled. "Is it the one on television? I don't want to be caught on camera in a tattoo shop."

Pixie raised her dark brows. "What are you, in witness protection or something? I mean, I like the hell out of you, Joy, but you sure are weird about getting spotted." Pixie pounded the table with her tiny fist. "No, wait, let me guess. You're a prolific bank robber. No? CIA agent?"

"No," Joy said, laughing. "None of the above, and you know it. I just... I'm just not interested in being on camera. I'll leave that to people who want it."

"Well, then you'll love Hawk. He hates Hollywood as a rule. I mean, he loves L.A., but he was always hiding out from the cameras when the show was on—which it isn't anymore, by the way. Explains why Hayley got so many guest spots and stuff. Hawk practically tossed her at the camera, not that she minded."

There was a slightly spiteful note in Pixie's voice and Joy surveyed her face for a long time before asking, "Do you like Hawk?"

Pixie's laughter floated around the room. "I do. Not the way you think, though. He's like my older brother. And just as annoying. All the women who walk into that shop are determined to sleep with him. He's super-hot, no shit, and all my friends want me to hook them up with him. But he's never interested in them, and so I get stuck in the middle."

"Ah, see? There's a good reason for me not to go. I'd hate to fall in love with him and beg for you to get me laid."

Joy couldn't suppress the grin that threatened, and Pixie howled laughter. "Of everyone I know, Joy, you'd be the last person I'd think would ask me to hook you up with him."

Joy said, "I don't know whether or not I should be insulted by that."

"You definitely shouldn't be." Pixie giggled. "But I have to tell you, of all my friends, you're the one I'd love to see with Hawk."

Joy's face heated. "Um, yeah. No. But thanks for thinking of me."

Pixie shrugged one shoulder, letting the camisole strap slide off it. "He's a good guy, Joy."

"I'm sure, but I'm not interested. Not into a tattoo, for obvious reasons, and not into meeting a guy, even if he is great."

Pixie smiled sympathetically. "You do know it's been a year, right? I mean, I know Brian hurt you, but I've seen guys hurt you before and you were never this bitter before."

Joy heaved a sigh. "I have every right to be."

Pixie shook her head. "Yeah, well...shit happens, you know? I don't mean that bad at all. I know it was rough on you when you found out what a louse Brian really is, but you shouldn't let it keep making you afraid to try again."

Brian.

Even his name made her heart hurt.

He'd been such a great guy. He'd been affectionate and caring, and chivalrous too. He never seemed to mind her small condo, or the fact that Pixie was usually camped out in the small spare room because she was constantly running out of money or 'forgetting' to pay her rent in favor of rescuing a dog, or cat, or ferret. Or a parrot.

Brian hadn't even seemed to mind the parrot, aptly named Caligula, who was currently sitting in his cage regarding her and Pixie with a looked of amused tolerance. Joy knew him well enough to know that expression was as deceptive as Brian had been.

He'd known, of course.

He'd known the entire time that she was one of Tyler Reed's daughters.

Tyler Reed, who'd started off as a small-time two-bit actor and gone on to become one of the most powerful producers and directors in Hollywood.

Joy was the product of his fourth marriage, and she'd been born when Tyler was in his late fifties. Unlike her sisters and brother, she wasn't cut out for the glare of the spotlight. Nor was she skinny, hooked on heroin or whatever designer drug was making the rounds, keen on hanging out in trendy nightclubs across the globe or shopping on Rodeo Drive, and she wasn't comfortable flashing credit cards at store clerks like the cards were garlic and the clerks vampires either. She hadn't had any DUIs. She had never failed at a marriage to rock star.

In other words, she was boring and ordinary. She was so unlike her half-siblings, who were and had done all of the above, that she'd managed to escape even being noticed.

She preferred things that way.

She'd gone to college on scholarships. She lived in a modest and inexpensive-for-L.A. condo in the flat side of Beverly Hills, the address mostly used by the struggling actors and musicians who were known to cram five or six people into a one-bedroom condo, and behind-the-scenes people who couldn't afford the more glamorous and hillier sections of the neighborhood.

She had a quiet job. A quiet life. Nobody knew who she was.

Except Brian had.

She should have realized he knew when he pretended he didn't want her for her. The bastard only wanted the opportunities he'd thought she could give him.

He was a struggling actor, and he'd worked at a very exclusive catering company for a while to make connections with actors and other Hollywood types. She'd met him at one of the parties her parents forced her to go to, and he'd literally charmed the pants right off her.

He'd not even mentioned that he was an actor for two weeks, and when he did she'd asked why he hadn't said so before, and his answer had been, "I didn't want you to think you had to help me."

That answer had clinched it. Suddenly she wanted to help him.

But he hadn't been content with her helping him to run lines for auditions or working on his expressions. He wanted to meet her father. He chafed at the fact that she had so many Hollywood-type networking connections and didn't use them. He'd pressed for her to go out with him and announce she was going out with him. He'd asked her to lease him a very expensive sports car, which she had said no to, of course. He'd demanded new clothes and head shots, and when she said no to financing those things he'd become sullen, moody, and cold. He'd even called in the paparazzi, not that they were the slightest bit interested, and then—when all those efforts on his part failed— he'd broken it off by telling her he would be better off dating anyone but her.

Caligula broke into her thoughts with, "Brian's a prick."

Pixie howled with laughter.

Joy sighed, unable to find the parrot funny. "How can a bird have better sense than me?"

Pixie stood and played with her gorgeous blue-dyed hair. "He's used to regarding people as the enemy. You aren't. Thank goodness! Or you were until after Brian, and I know he was the latest in string of guys who wanted you for what they thought you could give them instead of who you are, and that sucks; but hiding out here in the apartment all day isn't going to help you feel any better."

Joy retorted, "I'm not hiding."

Pixie shot back, "You aren't exactly out in plain sight either, and a day out of here would do you some good."

Joy crossed her arms and glared at Pixie. "I go out. I have client meetings and lunch dates with my folks, and I go shopping for groceries and..."

Pixie snorted. "That's not living, Joy. That's running errands. Besides, the pizza delivery guy is starting to get a crush on you. So you should probably get out and do something besides sit here and order pizza before he decides to fashion a wedding ring out of a garlic knot and propose or something."

Pixie had a point, as much as Joy didn't like to admit it. Brian hadn't been the first to leave her feeling used and with her self-esteem blown to bits, but she'd always managed to bounce back before.

And going to a tattoo shop wasn't the same as actually agreeing to a tattoo. She sighed. "Okay, I'll go. I'll even go to that restaurant you like."

Pixie clapped her hands and spun in a circle, sending the fluffed and floating layers of her skirt upward. "Yay! Now I don't have to kidnap you. Phew! I'm enough trouble over that hog thing."

Joy bit her lips. The day before, Pixie had climbed up on a semi hauling a load of live pigs and written "Help! Victims aboard!" in bright red letters across the rear end of it.

Joy ending up having to bail her out of jail, and while Pixie had been unrepentant, she'd also said that she wouldn't do it again.

Joy doubted that was true. "So what does one wear to a tattoo shop?"

Pixie ran her eyes over Joy's figure. Today she wore a soft white blouse with a neat little collar, blue jeans, and ballet flats. Her long blond hair was in a pretty fishtail braid and not a trace of makeup marred her fresh, creamy skin. "What you're wearing."

"Great. So I guess...um...what time?"

"Six," Pixie said as she smiled and jumped up and down. "And you can't try to wriggle out of it. You already promised." She vanished in the direction of her bedroom.

Caligula gave Joy a long stare and said, "Pixie's insane."

"Who you telling?" Joy countered. She shook her head and went to the kitchen to pour another cup of coffee before heading to her desk and the designs laid out across it.

She was an architect, and a damn good one. She didn't want to design fancy McMansions, or skyscrapers. She didn't want to design incredibly expensive shops either, although she did all those things so she could earn the money that would let her see her real dreams come true. She wanted to build eco-friendly homes for people who couldn't afford the homes that so many of her peers built.

She wanted to build earthquake-proof homes that would let in light and air and revitalize crumbling neighborhoods. The secret to it was finding materials she could use that would be less costly than the ones already in use, but still efficient, and ways to keep the costs down so the people in the neighborhoods she wanted to build in could actually afford them.

She'd seen revitalization price way too many right out of the homes they'd always known. She lived in a city, hell a whole state, where people were being priced out of middle-class neighborhoods and into unsafe ones because the upper-middle-class rents and house prices had soared beyond the reach of the people who lived there.

It was causing a major calamity, and people were being forced to leave their homes and schools and take on longer commutes as those with higher incomes started bidding wars in neighborhoods they would never have considered before, and the landlords, fueled by greed and the rising tides, gleefully charged in with rent increases and minor cosmetic renovations to bring those people into the neighborhoods whose people were being forced to vacate.

It was a shitty mess as far as Joy was concerned, and it hit her that the answer was to revitalize the lower-income neighborhoods while keeping the prices down, so those who'd been priced out of their own neighborhoods could find decent and safe housing, while those already in those neighborhoods could take part in rebuilding it.

Nobody believed she could pull any of it off.

She loved Earthcraft homes, but they were horrendously expensive to build, and she was researching materials that would give the same kind of tight building envelope while having a lower cost when Pixie swept back out.

"Hey there, you ready to go?"

Joy looked up, blinking. "Huh?"

"The tattoo shop."

"Oh, right. Um, yeah. Let me just close this down." She rubbed her eyes and shut the laptop off and neatly stacked her designs.

"How's it going?" She'd freshened her makeup and done something with her hair to make it even prettier.

Joy rubbed her neck with one hand. "Meh. I don't know. I know there's a simple solution somewhere; I just have to find it."

"You will," Pixie said reassuringly.

Joy wasn't so sure, but she was glad Pixie at least had some faith in her.

The tattoo shop settled in between a small strip of stores and it looked packed. Joy, getting out of the car, paused for a moment, her forehead wrinkling. She hated big crowds, as she always felt awkward in them.

Pixie headed for the shop and Joy followed slowly. She caught sight of her reflection in the tinted windows of a sex store and sighed inwardly.

In a sea of bone-thin women who practiced yoga and juicing, she stuck out like a plump thumb.

She had wide shoulders thanks to years of swimming, rounded arms and legs, and stubborn curves of hip and breasts that, no matter how many crash diets her mother had tried out on her, just wouldn't slim down or vanish.

When she'd been young she'd been forced into dance classes, aerobics, and every other workout class under the sun. She'd done Pilates, yoga, water aerobics, and run for miles on treadmills, but her thighs stayed thick and her hips stayed wide, to her mother's utter despair.

The plant-based, low-fat, sugar-free, low-calorie diet that her mother, Megan, a former model and actress, ate kept her and Joy's father lean and fit, and she was sure that it was all her growing daughter needed for her body to suddenly go from thick and wide to tall and elegant. It hadn't worked.

Joy would eat the meager meals they offered her, and go to bed with her stomach growling and her head aching. Thankfully by the time she was in junior high school, she'd discovered she could actually throw away the sprouted grain and bean sprout sandwiches Megan stuffed into her lunch box in favor of food bought at the school cafeteria, and she had.

She knew a size twelve wasn't obese. She knew her size was actually average everywhere else in the country but in L.A., the land of film and money, it was unacceptable, and she was often the brunt of body- shaming jokes that left her feeling exposed and hurt.

She set aside those thoughts as they entered the building. The first thing she noticed was the number of people, and she immediately gravitated toward the nearest wall. She had thought to feign interest in the art displayed up there, but soon found herself fascinated; not by the photographs of tattoos and the flash art, but by the paintings, neatly framed, that hung here and there.

They weren't signed, but they were very good. They showed L.A. as it was. Real people on street corners in bad neighborhoods, the crumbling Hollywood sign, a woman running down a street, her face creased in concentration and earbuds dangling.

A smile crossed her mouth as she continued to survey the paintings. She was so engrossed she didn't even notice to the handsome guy coming out of his work station to greet Pixie until she heard Pixie speak.

She turned and her heart leaped into her throat. Pixie had said he was hot. She hadn't said he was drop- dead gorgeous, but damn, he was.

The heavy tattoos on his arms only added to his looks, and his thickly-lashed green eyes slid over to her as Pixie hugged the stranger.

"Meet Joy. My bestie. She saved my ass yesterday. Made my bail and everything. Joy, this is Hawk: My back-up bail-bond boy." Pixie grinned and punched Hawk playfully in the ribs.

Hawk laughed and asked, "What did you do now?"

Joy stared at him as Pixie began to explain.

"Hold on a sec," Joy interrupted Pixie. "You're telling it wrong." She shrugged and rolled her eyes at Hawk. "Does she try that on you too?"

He grinned and nodded. "Truth, Pix. Nothing but the truth."

Joy laughed at Pixie's feigned expression of disappointment. "Let me try," Joy said and proceeded to explain the whole spray-painting-the-hog-truck debacle. There was a sudden pounding in her chest and a flush of heat running through her body as she watched Hawk. He was muscular but lean, and there was an aura of street tough hanging off him like a mist. She was drawn to it, and to him.

She swallowed hard as Hawk said, "So your vegetarian leanings got you landed in jail, huh?"

Pixie glowered at him. "They were innocent little piggies, Hawk. Someone had to speak out. I don't know why everyone doesn't go vegetarian. You should try it too; it's good for you, and the planet."

Hawk ran a hand through his sooty hair and grinned. "I would be a vegetarian if I could, but there's always something standing between me and a vegetarian diet."

Pixie asked, "What?"

"Bacon," Hawk said. "It's delicious."

Joy burst into laughter. She couldn't help it. Hawk smiled at her, revealing square white teeth and a small dimple in his right cheek. Her heart pounded even harder, threatening to cause her to crumple to the floor in an embarrassing heap.

"Sorry," he said in a voice that said he wasn't sorry at all. "But bacon is *really* good."

"Oh, I agree. I love bacon. I'd eat bacon wrapped in bacon if you let me." Immediately her face flushed. She was flirting! And, what was more, she was a big girl talking about food. Thin women could joke about how much they ate, not women who wore a size twelve.

Hawk grinned at her. "Hell, I have. I once ate—"

Pixie threw her hands up. "Okay, that's enough! I'll have both your hides if you try teasing me." She pretended to look sternly at both of them, the corners of her mouth giving away her secret. "Hey, Hawk? Do you have time to work on my leg?"

"I do." His eyes stayed on Joy's. Her face grew even hotter. Hawk's glance trailed down her arms. "Are you interested in a tat?"

She shook her head. There was a real and physical reason she couldn't get a tattoo, but she was not about to tell him, or anyone, that. "Oh, no. No thank you. Not for me. I mean...I mean I like them...on other people. They're nice, I just..." She was just digging herself in even deeper, so she stopped and pointed behind Hawk, then rushed on, "I love these paintings. Do you know the artist? Who did them?"

"I did."

The words made her blink. She looked from him back to the paintings. "They're fantastic."

"Thanks. Most people don't pay attention to them."

"Well I doubt you could tattoo that one on skin with as much success. Photorealism is a hard thing to accomplish on canvas."

"This is true." His voice was a silky caress. It slid across her skin, and left her shivering and even more mute, and embarrassed. The reaction was odd and disconcerting, and she wasn't sure she hated it, but she was pretty sure she didn't like it.

It left her too bared and exposed.

Pixie chirped up, "Do you have any more of the really pretty violet ink?"

Hawk turned to look at her and the spell shattered and scattered around Joy, but she still felt a remnant of the shivering and heat low in her belly.

They went into his work room and Hawk, pointing to a small stool in the corner, said to Joy, "Take a seat over there."

Pixie hopped up on the table and stuck her left leg out to reveal the half-finished gorgeous tattoo. Joy watched, fascinated, as Hawk carefully took tools out of an enclave and then opened a pack with a fresh tattoo needle inside.

He put on latex gloves, and then spurted Hibiclens across Pixie's leg, wiping it quickly with a disinfectant-laden paper towel. He took a pink razor from a pack, took off the plastic guard, and shaved her leg rapidly then bagged the razor and cap and disposed of it.

It was a lot more sanitary than she had imagined, and better lit too. She'd imagined some dim and creepy place, garish with neon and rough-looking people all sporting Mohawks or biker gear. She'd seen a few Mohawks and some biker gear, but for the most part they all seemed to be just normal people.

Pixie sat still while Hawk worked.

Joy wanted to talk but she was afraid if she did she would distract him. Instead she watched his steady hand applying the needle, which whirred and spun beneath the gun. She let her gaze shift upwards. His face was set in lines of concentration and his mouth, full and generous, was pressed into a slightly flatter line as he pulled the gun away, examined the work he'd done so far, and then continued.

Eventually it was finished. Hawk carefully wrapped a bandage around Pixie's slender leg and said, "There you go."

She looked down at the bandage, the white swath of it a bright blot against her skin. "Thanks! Joy and I are going out for dinner at the Green House; you want to go?"

"No." His lips twitched. "My body automatically rejects anything even remotely healthy these days."

Pixie glared at him.

Hawks lips trembled, then he burst into laughter. Joy wanted to laugh too but she wasn't sure if she should. Hawk nodded and ruffled Pixie's hair. "Yeah, I'll go. In fact, I'll pay. It isn't every day I get to take two women out."

Joy doubted that. She could tell he was used to being around women, and he had a kind of smooth and sexy confidence that came naturally to him too. That and his good looks probably made him damn near irresistible.

For most women.

Not for her.

She could definitely resist him.

Because he was obviously not interested in her anyway.

CHAPTER 3

Hawk stared; he tried not to, but he couldn't help himself. The woman in from of him had him slightly rattled. Joy, Pixie's best bud, was not only beautiful, but she had this sort of innocence and vulnerability literally dripping off her that appealed to him so much it had taken everything he had not to hit on her. *Damn!*

She was curvy and lush, her body a perfect hourglass with stunning, sleek skin; the kind of woman so rare in L.A. it was akin to walking out of his work room and seeing a unicorn suddenly appear in the shop.

She also had this amazing, shy, sweet smile, made even more tempting by her gloriously blue eyes. He wanted to kiss her full bottom lip and nibble on it until she opened her mouth. He bet she knew how to kiss. The kind that took your breath away.

Joy sat quietly in the chair, not talking, just watching intently as he tattooed Pixie. He was aware of the weight of her gaze in a way he'd never cared about before. It took extra concentration on Pixie's leg just to get the job done; all the while his mind ran through imaginary scenarios of him and Joy alone, stripping her down and making love to her. That woman sitting in the swivel chair wasn't made for sex, she was made for love. It terrified and excited him at the same time.

He was tempted to say no to dinner. Pixie was undoubtedly going to stuff him full of some crazy vegetable-and-soy-laden stuff, and he'd have to sit there trying to choke down the awful stuff while trying to think of something witty and charming to say to Joy, when all he really wanted to do was stare at her.

That irritated him a little. Okay, maybe a lot.

He wasn't used to being so stricken and smitten, and he also wasn't used to being confused about whether or not a woman was interested in him. He thought he saw something in her eyes, but her expression was so veiled it was almost impossible to tell. It frustrated him, as did his tongue's sudden cleaving to the roof of his mouth every time he tried to open his mouth to say something to her while he was tattooing Pixie, who was also suddenly silent, which wasn't like her at all. He needed her to fill the space with her quirky jabber.

Joy intrigued him in ways he hadn't been in a long time, and by the time he met them at the restaurant he was determined to talk to her.

The restaurant served both vegetarian and meat options, and when Joy ordered a steak, medium-rare, he smiled and closed the menu. "I'll have the same," he said.

Pixie ordered some concoction, and when the server left Pixie asked, "So how was your day, Hawk?"

He grimaced. "I had to tattoo Jack Monroe."

Joy asked, "Who's that?"

He grinned. "He's a pop singer and a giant pain in the ass."

"He is? If you didn't want to work on him, couldn't you have said no?"

Hawk smiled, loving the sound of her voice, "I do have a no list and he's on it, but my new receptionist didn't know. Totally my fault. I should've made sure she did. So, to answer your question, before you came in with Pixie, my work room was taken over by bodyguards and hangers-on, along with a few groupies, one of whom attempted to ease the singer's pain by offering him a blowjob."

Pixie said, "Ouch." She giggled. "Sounds like the perfect day."

Hawk rolled his eyes. "Yeah, you know me so well, Pix." He turned back to the gorgeous blue eyes across from him and explained, "I don't dislike most Hollywood types, but that kid..." He shook his head.

Joy's eyes met his and stayed there. "Do you get a lot of Hollywood types?"

Crap. Was she an actress or in the business? "Some," he said cautiously. Had he sounded too annoyed by all A-listed Hollywood people?

"I see." She looked away and stared at the people inside the restaurant.

He couldn't figure her out so he asked, "I know what Pixie does, but what about you?"

"Oh. I'm an architect. I..." She licked her lips; a tantalizing flash of her pink tongue showed against the darker pink flesh of her mouth for a moment and then she continued, "I want to revitalize lower-income neighborhoods without causing anymore disturbance in the already-unfair and unbalanced rental and housing markets." She shrugged and smiled, almost apologetically. "I know how that must sound..."

"Logical?"

"Impossible." She sighed and picked at the edges of her napkin. "It's a mess, and everyone knows why, but they all keep overlooking the simplest solutions. The issue is that with the housing boom and bust a lot of people in higher-income neighborhoods find themselves having to move. They pick the next-best neighborhoods, naturally."

He set his elbow on the table and rested his chin on his hand, clearly intrigued. "Go on, please."

"They move into neighborhoods with lower prices, for them, but those prices get driven up higher because of their arrival, and the people in the neighborhoods that they moved into, as a consequence, find themselves priced out. *They* move and now they're all moving and continuing that cycle in other neighborhoods."

"And nobody wins. Except maybe the landlords and developers." Hawk was beyond impressed. "So what's your plan?"

"Revitalization at low cost; restoring civic pride and keeping people in their own neighborhoods. The issue is that if we revitalize, then those neighborhoods become more attractive to those priced out elsewhere, so what I'd like to see is the ability for more people to actually buy instead of just renting. To do that, there needs to be revitalization, to make those homes attractive to the people in them to purchase them, and to feel like staying in a neighborhood that they have been working to get out of is really the place they want to be."

"It also gives them an anchor in their neighborhoods. It's hard to price-out owners." Hawk shook his head and straightened when he saw the waiter coming with trays in his hand.

Their food arrived and as they dug in, Pixie said, "She's been working on this since college. It used to drive her professors crazy. She has these plans to create green space with recycled materials like tires and plastic bottles and stuff."

Even more impressed, Hawk stared at the smart, beautiful woman across from him. "You really care about this."

She gave him a shy smile. "I do. I just don't have a lot of logistical answers. The truth is that the revitalization needs the cooperation of the neighborhood. The people have to be willing to buy in. For many that means working on credit issues and saving money at a time when things are already stretched really thin. But it can be done, and the only way to really fuel their wanting to buy in is to give them something to buy into."

Hawk bit into a tender chunk of steak. "How do you plan to do that?"

She looked sheepish. "Buy a few houses and renovate. Fund green space out of my pocket, give the neighborhood an idea of what it could be like with revitalization. Make it something they want to fight for. I can't repair credit or income issues, but there are plenty of lenders willing to work with them. The rest is up to them."

He gawked at her then said, "Holy shit, you really do believe in this."

She nodded. Her smile got wider. "Go big or go home, right?"

He grinned. "That's how I've always looked at it."

She started to eat, and he watched her while chatting with Pixie about mutual friends. Joy ate slowly, obviously enjoying the food, but with a notable self-consciousness too. He could guess what that stemmed from.

The conversation eased into other channels, and long before he wanted it to be, dinner was over.

"Thanks for the invite, Pix," Hawk said and smiled at his little buddy before giving her a big hug. "I had a good time." He turned to Joy and tried not to stare to hard into her pretty blue eyes. "It was nice meeting you as well." He held out his hand, and when her soft, warm fingers curled around his palm, he had to mentally tell himself not to pull her into a tight hug or try to kiss her. He was sure it was written all over his face.

"Good-night, Hawk." Her voice, soft and husky, seemed to carry a hint of something as she said his name. He couldn't quite figure out what.

He nodded and pointed at Pix. "You keep an eye on that new tattoo. Let me know if there're any problems or something you don't like."

She playfully punched him in his hard abs. "You know it's perfect. It always is."

After smiling and standing there a little too long, he reluctantly turned and headed to his bike. He nodded once more as he passed the two beautiful ladies and headed home. The bike tooled along the highway and he smiled at the sensation of the powerful engine below and the wind in his hair.

Joy stayed in his thoughts as he pulled up in front of his modest house. He'd grown up in a rough neighborhood, so he knew exactly what she was talking about.

When houses and rent became too high in the more desirable areas, people with more money did move in, and brought their money with them. Families with less money didn't just get priced-out; their kids had to handle a sudden influx of kids used to more who were bitter and angry at their sudden shifting into a new place. They formed their own cliques, and their clothes and money set them up as little princes and princesses, and they knew it.

He opened the gate and drove through it. The house was simple, a small 1950 post-and-beam place, with large windows that looked out over the miniscule yard and infinity pool. His home was filled with character, along with his art and other things he'd bought over the years. It was his, just like the shop. He'd gotten them through hard work and struggle.

He headed into the kitchen and pulled out a bottle of wine, then opened it and poured himself a generous amount. His eyes wandered over the quartz counters and stainless steel appliances and, as he always did, he found himself comparing the house to the small, rundown home he'd lived in as a child.

He had hardwood on his floors, and the torn linoleum of his youth was now gone. The grimy windows and stained walls groaning under a heavy freight of whatever paint was cheaper had been replaced by the clean, white expanses of walls thicker than any he'd known as a kid.

Hawk knew part of his public reputation came from his having been raised in such a tough neighborhood, and that while that added to his street cred, it also hindered him too. He wanted success, but he wanted it his way. He wasn't running from his past, but he wasn't willing to stay where he had been either.

Most of the guys he'd gone to high school with had washed up and out, ending up on drugs or working at jobs they hated. There were a few exceptions, most notably John, who'd taken their football-playing in junior high and high school into a good college program, where he'd gotten his degree in business.

He was as good with accounting as he had been as a defensive player and was now Hawk's financial manager; and he was the one person Hawk could always count on not to bullshit him about how the shop was doing. And now it was doing spectacularly. He'd saved his money religiously in order to open it, and he'd done that so he wouldn't have to take out loans he might not be able to pay back.

In the end, the lean years of interning and working hard had paid off, and he was proud of all that he accomplished. He had everything he wanted.

Except a woman to share it all with.

Which just took him right back to Joy. Again.

CHAPTER 4

"He likes you." Pixie's words cut through the silence that had built in the car.

Joy, navigating past a thick clump of traffic, didn't turn her head as she said, "What?"

"Hawk." There was amusement in Pixie's voice. "He likes you. I can tell."

Joy's belly fluttered but she said, "I liked him too. He seems like a nice guy. Not quite what I pictured a tattoo artist to be like."

Pixie crowed with rich laughter. "Nice? Hawk? No. But he's a good man anyway. And when I say he liked you I meant he liked you as a woman. Not just as a person."

Heat crept into Joy's face. "No, he didn't."

"He does."

Choosing her words carefully, Joy said, "Well, I'm sure he isn't interested in me, and even if he was I wouldn't want to step on your toes."

"Crap. You really need to get out more!" Pixie played with her short blue hair. "There's nothing between me and Hawk, and you would know that if you were around people more instead of hiding away in the apartment, sketching up designs for your utopia and your rich clients' McMansions."

"Hey now, those rich clients are going to pay for Utopia." Joy grinned and then turned her thoughts back to Hawk, her smile disappearing. "I'm sure you're wrong, Pixie. Guys don't like girls like me, and you know it." A world of hurt lay beneath her voice.

Pixie obviously heard it too. "Joy, not every guy is an ass. Not every guy wants a toothpick-thin woman, either."

"Yeah? Let me know when you have to navigate the world as me, and we'll discuss that."

"Ouch. Are you telling me to check my privilege?"

Joy bit her lips. "I'm saying you've never been my size, so you don't understand."

"That would be a yes then. You're right. I am thin, and naturally so. I've never had to handle rude jerks who think me unworthy because I can't fit into a size two." Pixie put a warm hand on her arm. "I won't pretend I know what's like to have that happen, and since I have seen it happen to you I get that it hurts you. But you are not fat. Or obese. Or overweight. None of that. You get that, right?"

Joy shrugged. She didn't feel overweight, or obese. She just felt... big. She towered over Pixie.

"I also get that you're not just dealing with a stupid idealized beauty standard, but dealing with guys who want you because they imagine one day you'll come away with some of those millions and give it to them. Or help them with their careers."

Joy swallowed hard. "Well, that's just the way it is. We're all labelled," she said, and thought about Hawk and what she had thought he was like before she had even met him, "and we're all guilty of labelling. Can we talk about something else?"

She knew Pixie meant well. They'd met their first year at college, and they'd become fast friends and roommates too, and even now, six years after college had released them, they were still friends. They might not see each other every day, but they'd been there for each other through a lot of things, and she was always grateful to have such a good friend, but, no, Pixie didn't get it.

Pixie was a what-you-see-is-what-you-get kind of person. She'd grown up in a solidly blue-collar Midwestern home, and she was sensible and kind, and flighty and weird. She was also stunningly beautiful and she could eat her weight in cookies and never gain a single pound.

Joy pulled into her parking spot and the two of them got out and headed inside.

Pixie snapped her fingers. "Oh, change of subject; did I tell you I'm going up to Napa tomorrow?"

Joy blinked. "No."

"Yeah I decided to go hang out with Laurie and Josh for a couple of days. You want to come?"

Joy shook her head, regretfully. "No, but I wish I could. I've a huge deadline looming and I'm nowhere near close to getting it done. I'll have to work overtime until it finished."

"No problem. You know the invite's open if you change your mind." Pixie yawned and stretched. "I'm beat and, what's more, my binge shows are on. You want to watch?"

Joy smiled. "No. I know how you are. You'll be throwing popcorn and screaming at the screen."

"Yes, it's all true, Your Honor." She grinned and added, "I have to get up at five to catch my ride, so I'll probably crash early. I'll bring you back some good vino."

"Chardonnay," Joy said firmly.

Pixie gave her a hug and skipped off to her room, her dress floating up around her legs while Joy sat down and stared down at the plans she'd been working on earlier. Normally she could focus like a laser, but tonight she was restless.

Hawk.

He was definitely sexy as all hell.

And funny.

And successful in his own way and right.

The perfect man.

Only, a man that perfect was probably not ever going to be interested in a woman who was, to put it mildly, insecure and introverted. She knew she was being too hard on herself. She had a lot to offer; she just had to find the right person to offer it too, and that person wasn't Hawk.

But, damn, he was tempting.

Pixie was long gone when Joy woke up. She headed down to the gym for half an hour and came back up and showered quickly. She dressed comfortably and settled down at her desk to work on the deadline project she needed to finish. Unfortunately, she had a hard time concentrating.

Her mind kept going back to Hawk.

She was being ridiculous. The man likely had women lined up for miles, and he'd probably already forgotten all about her.

If only she could forget about him!

She couldn't, though. She found herself thinking of the art up on the walls of his shop, and the way his hands had been so steady as he plied the needle across Pixie's flesh.

Frustrated by her inability to concentrate, or even think, she headed out of her place. As much as she hated to do it, she'd promised to have lunch with her mother. It wouldn't hurt to be early. She got in her car and gave her reflection a quick peek. She'd applied a minimal amount of mascara and gloss, and a slight dusting of a fine mineral powder foundation to cover the faint dark circles under her eyes. Those dark circles were due to her tossing and turning all night in a restlessness she had absolutely no clue how to handle.

She was used to being content with her life and being alone, with the occasional exception of Pixie and Caligula. "Thank goodness Pixie took that damn bird with her," she muttered and then grinned, wondering how long it would be before Caligula drove Pixie's hosts nuts with his one-line insults and ability to poop right through the bars of a cage and onto the floor, or, more recently, right onto the hapless person who happened to be anywhere near his cage.

Pixie swore Caligula would be her next boyfriend's litmus test. If the bird liked him, he was okay. Joy had to admit, ruefully, that

Pixie might have a point. Caligula had spent hours insulting Brian, and look how he'd turned out.

Traffic was light at that time of the day. Rodeo Drive, in the early mornings and afternoon, was the haunt of tourists and tour buses, and the tourists who were out were wandering along, stunned and confused, as they looked around the sun-washed streets in hopes of catching a glimpse of some celebrity strolling out of the mostly silent shops and eateries.

She parked in a garage and headed into the place her mother had told her to meet her. She walked along the concrete sidewalk, mindlessly window-shopping, seeing the high-priced name brands of purses and clothes, not missing that she never shopped in them. The minute she walked into the door of the restaurant, she wanted to leave.

Megan Reed lounged in a chair, her slim and elegant frame covered in off-white linen. Her hair, a perfect honey blonde, hung over one shoulder in a thick and exquisite braid. Her makeup was flawless, and at her elbow sat a tall glass of water that had likely been infused with either asparagus or some other green vegetable or fruit.

Across from her sat Lily, Joy's half-sister.

Lily, fresh off her third divorce, this one a shattered mess created by a cheating, drug-addicted rock star of an ex, was just as impeccably groomed.

Her frame was lean like Megan's, and, like her stepmother she, too, had been a model. Lily's black hair was drawn straight back from her tall forehead, and her perfectly arched eyebrows formed a double crescent as she took in Joy.

Joy forced a smile and headed for the table.

Lily's eyes grew wide as she stared at Joy. "Are you ill?"

"No." Joy snuck a peek at the water next to Megan's hand. Definitely slightly green.

Megan continued to stare. "You look tired. Like *really* tired."

Already. She hadn't even managed to order a drink yet and they were insulting her. Joy pressed her lips in a tight line. "I've been working a lot."

"I worked a lot as a model," Megan said in a reproving tone. "Tell her, Lily, about when we had fifteen- hour and longer days, not to mention flights before and after. Now that was hard work, and we had to get off work looking as fresh as we had when we went in. Try some rose hip oil. It'll perk your skin up."

Joy pretended to make a mental note. "Will do." Had her mother ever been kind to her? She felt like Cinderella sometimes, with Lily being the real daughter and she just the stepchild.

She couldn't remember her mother ever being sweet. She could remember growing up in the shadows of the stunning Lily and the equally stunning Rose, and Calla. She had never measured up and she'd often had the uneasy feeling that her mother would have been quite happy if she could just claim her stepdaughters as her own, and ship her biological daughter off somewhere, never to be seen again. Forcing the thought aside, she asked, "Is Dad coming?"

Her mother checked the expensive watch on her wrist. "He's supposed to be. Would you like some oxygen-infused water?"

"Yes, thank you." What she really wanted a good hard bolt of liquor. Or a rocket ship that would take her right out of there.

Megan beckoned a waiter over. "A glass of oxy water with ice, please. Oh, and we'll go ahead and order an appetizer to share. The steamed edamame, no salt please."

Yup. It just kept getting worse.

Joy wished she'd grabbed something to snack on before coming to lunch. "How's the reality show going, Lily?"

Lily sipped her water and pouted. "Okay. The ratings could be better. The divorce really drove them up, so of course now we're seeing a slight slump."

Divorce, reduced to ratings. Lily had two kids, and an ex who had publicly humiliated her. But never mind the pain and heartache and the kids' feelings. Worry about the ratings. When had her family become the Kardashians?

Joy was still trying to process that when her father, the infamous Tyler Blake, appeared. He greeted his wife and daughter before turning to his youngest daughter.

"Sweetie!" A genuine smile filled his face as he took the seat across from her and asked, "How's your project going, Joy?"

"Which one?"

He gave her a fond smile. "The paying one. And the other too, of course."

"They're both good." She snorted and tried to cover the sound when her mother shot her a disapproving frown. "I'm enjoying the challenges of them both, anyway."

The server appeared again and took Tyler's drink order, then handed out the menus while her mother said, "I ordered steamed edamame. I know you hate them, but I figured we girls could pick at them while we wait for lunch."

Joy had no intention of eating the edamame. She hated it. Pixie would have scarfed down the whole dish and asked for more.

Lunch progressed at its usual torturous pace. Joy was exhausted and bored long before her simple green salad and grilled shrimp appeared, and she seriously considering excusing herself too.

Lily cleared her throat loudly, catching their attention. "I'm considering doing something to boost ratings," and then cut a miniscule bite off the end of one of her shrimp.

Tyler sighed. "I don't know why you can't just put that damn show to bed. I realize the pay's good, and I applaud your being willing to do reality television, but, really, you're wasting your talent. The days of reality stars going mainstream are long over."

She set her fork down and leaned over. "Well, Father, you could put me in one of your films."

"Then I'd be accused of nepotism," he said calmly.

"It's Hollywood. Everything's some sort of nepotism."

Tyler took a long swallow of his whiskey and said firmly, "I just don't have a part for you, Lily."

It was an old argument that would never end.

Joy squirmed, uncomfortable and anxious, in her chair. She pressed Lily, "What're you going to do to boost ratings?" She said it not because she cared, but she simply wanted to stave off any more of their jousting. She knew from long experience it would disintegrate quickly into a shouting match, and she wanted nothing to do with that. Especially in public. Lily probably had a crew of cameras hiding out around the corner, ready to start filming the moment their voices raised.

Lily brushed an imaginary speck of dust off her blouse. "I'm going to try to get that tattoo artist, the super-hot one who used to have that show, Fly High Tattoos, to come on my show."

"Hawk?" The words were out before she meant to speak them.

Lily stared at her dismissively. "I didn't know you watched that show. Yes, Hawk. I think I'm going to try to talk him into a little cameo and let the editors and so on turn it into a 'did they or didn't they?' kind of storyline. Ratings will pick up, and in a week or two I could show off some fake tattoo on my derrière or something."

"No tattoos, Lily." The tone in their father's voice showed them he meant it.

All Joy could do was stare at her half-sister. "That's... I mean...you can't do that!"

One of Lily's smooth bronzed shoulders lifted and dropped. "Why not? Mark, that bastard, was always in his shop getting fresh ink, and he cheated on me at the shop too. It would make the show interesting, and he's so hot."

"He wouldn't appreciate being taken advantage of. He's very nice."

Lily smirked. "On-camera I'm sure he is."

Joy clenched her fork. "Off-camera too."

"Oh, do tell." Lily lifted a brow and leaned forward. "Wait! How would you know?"

"I had dinner with him last night." Her face burned as Lily's eyes narrowed and then sharpened. "Pixie's a friend of his and we, all three of us, had dinner last night. It wasn't a date."

Lily sniffed again. "Of course not. Nobody suggested it was. Trust me there." She looked at Joy's mother and gave her a knowing look.

Joy's anger hit hard. Nobody would have suggested that, of course not. Not one of them could imagine a man like Hawk wanting anything at all to do with her. Lily, yes. Her, no. That same old lack of self-esteem and insecurity rolled through her, shredding her defenses. Her eyes watered but she blinked back whatever moisture was there.

Her father broke in, his voice soft as he said, "Drop it, Lily. Having him on your show is not going to fly. Leave it alone."

Joy met her father's gaze. He'd always been kind to her, and she smiled gratefully at him. He just resumed eating.

"Next you'll say you got a tattoo," Lily said silkily. "Although why anyone would is beyond me. I'm not about to destroy my skin with something so tacky. Can you imagine what it will look like in a decade? Then again, you never really did care much about your looks."

Joy retrained the urge to grab Lily by her hair and slam her head into the table. Lily had always been mean to her.

Always.

Hadn't she just said she would have people think she got a tattoo for the show?

Her mother tapped her manicured finger on the table. She had always said it was normal for her half-sisters to be angry at her. She'd never explained why they were so mean to Joy, but they really did love her. After a while it had become painfully obvious. Joy was nothing like them, and they knew it. She was a dodo bird dropped into a nest of swans.

Joy spoke clearly as she tossed her napkin on the table. She could take a lot, but Lily was being ridiculous, and she refused to put up with it any longer. "Lily, listen because I'm only going to say this once. I earn my living through my brains and talent. If I wanted a tattoo, I'd get one, and it wouldn't change how much money I make. You don't understand this, but I'm three-hundred-percent better off than you. Heaven forbid if you gain a pound, or get a pimple, or a gray hair, or fart in public; your entire livelihood and life may be ruined. So, no, I don't pay attention to my looks. I don't need them to get through my life. But then again, you pay enough attention to yours for the both of us. I guess lacking everything else, you sort of have to." She'd never said anything even remotely rude like that to her siblings. She was trembling with anger, and she was also hungry. The tiny salad was as appetizing as dirt. She lifted a hand and when the waiter appeared, she said, "This is awful. Bring me the pasta carbonara, and a glass of Chardonnay. Oh, and bread. Garlic. Please."

The waiter hid a grin, nodded, and quickly took off.

Her mother frowned. "Joy, that's going to wreck your figure."

"I'm sure it won't," she returned sharply. "I'm a grown woman. I'll eat what I want." She stared at her mother. "And I'd stop frowning, Mother. It'll put lines on your face."

The waiter came back shortly with her food, breaking into the tense silence.

Her mother watched her eat a few bites and spoke, in a slightly timid tone, "Would you like to go shopping with us after lunch?"

"No, thank you. I need to get back to work."

"And the tattoo shop?" Lily said angry. Her red-tipped nails tapped the table in measured little thunks that set Joy's nerves on edge.

"That too." Was she going to get a tattoo? Well, why the hell not? She'd only been against it because of what her father would think. He didn't seem to care. He was more interested in his phone than them.

A sense of recklessness filled her. Then it quickly died. A tattoo would mean broken skin, and blood. She couldn't do it.

But maybe there was something she could do.

Soon after, her mother and Lily left to going shopping. The mood had become too tense and Joy could feel the two of them blame her. When the left, her father picked up his fork and stabbed at the pasta on her plate and ate it. He grinned and winked at her. "Don't tell your mom."

"I won't." She laughed, instantly relaxing. "You want some bread too?"

He eyed the thick buttery slice, "Do you think she'll smell it on my breath?"

Joy spoke bluntly. "You two barely speak, and you have separate bedrooms. Do you really think she's getting close enough to smell your breath?"

He set the fork down and said, "Damn it! You're right."

She shook her head and gave him a supportive smile. "Why do you stay married, Daddy? If you're not happy..."

The childish name slid past her lips before she could stop it. Her father picked up the fork again and took her plate, grabbing another mouthful of pasta. "I'm in my eighties. She's still beautiful, and young. Young next to me, anyway. We've been together nearly thirty years. It's hard to leave what you know."

"I guess." She did understand better than she let on. Sometimes it was easier than dealing with change. He was right.

"So are you going to tell me about this Hawk boy?'

She cupped her elbows. "Why?"

"Why?" he mimicked her in a sweet teasing tone then returned to his regular voice, "Because I have never seen you lay into Lily like that, and she's deserved it for years. And I have never seen you order pasta in front of your mother either." He grinned. "I'm proud of you, girl. Baby steps, but in the right direction."

She pointed out, "You don't order pasta in front of her."

"Nobody in their right mind would," he chuckled. "Now stop skirting the subject; what's going on with this man that you felt the need to keep him away from Lily?"

She shook her head and reached for her glass of water. "It's not that. He's...I mean we aren't. I just met him, and he's very nice. Sweet actually. If Lily gets her claws into him... I don't think it's fair to screw with people's lives like that."

"I see," Tyler nibbled at the garlic bread. "Have you seen your other sisters lately?"

"No. How are they?"

"Rose is apparently having a great time living in Malibu and blowing her trust fund, and Call's working on a fashion line. Purses. She should be able to design those well enough. Heaven knows she buys enough of them."

Joy didn't want to ask but she did. "How's Max?"

Her father gave her a shrewd stare. "Enjoying his latest rehab, from what I hear. He's in there with...what was the Lily's last husband's name?"

"Mark," she supplied.

"Mark." He set the crust of bread aside. "I'm proud of you, Joy. More than any of the others, I'm proud of you. I love all my kids, but you—you I'm proud of. You're the only one who never wanted anything from me. Hell, you wouldn't even take college tuition. You had to go on your scholarships and work at those shitty little bartending jobs. I used to try to think of ways to give you money on the sly that you wouldn't know was from me."

"I didn't need it."

He smiled. "No, you didn't. What do you say we split a piece of cheesecake?"

She wanted to, but also knew he wasn't supposed to have the sugar. "I say if you died any time soon I'd never stop blaming myself. And neither would anyone else."

"You've got a good point there."

She nodded. "Are you okay?"

"Yes, just really busy. I'm thinking of retiring this year. It would be nice to just relax and enjoy what I've earned."

"Everyone else has enjoyed it so, yeah, you should too." She grinned.

"They're your family, Joy."

"And I want you to spend all our inheritance on yourself. You deserve it... we don't." She twisted her hands together, trying to think of how to put her feelings into words that wouldn't sting. She settled for, "I know they're my family and I want to love them, but...but they don't seem to care much for me."

He didn't argue, only nodded, "I can see that. Your mom does love you..."

"She's disappointed in me." It was true. They both knew it.

"You have to understand her, sweetie. She's used to being around women who make their names and fortune by being beautiful. You scare the hell out of her. It's not the other way around. You were always determined to do something else, and then..."

"When she figured out I was going to be a thick-figured girl," Joy added sarcastically.

"No! When you started doing things she couldn't understand or compete with, like talking about college when you were in sixth grade, and winning awards for essays and projects at school, she got even more scared. You went your own way, and every time you came home with some academic honor or new achievement, she got more and more certain that you saw her as stupid and superficial. Lily sees your mom as successful and important, but you...she's afraid you'll never see her anything more than a clothes hanger."

"I don't see her like that at all!" She appreciated that her father was trying to explain how her mother felt, but still... "She's not very nice to me, and there's not any excuse for that."

Her father swirled the ice in his drink, but said nothing.

She couldn't believe she'd said those thoughts out loud and to admit it to her father... she wasn't surprised he had nothing to say. "I get that I'm not what she expected. I get that I'm not anyone she understands, but that's not my fault! She could try to understand me."

"And you have no reason to try to understand her?" he asked quietly.

Her face flushed. "Ouch. True. Sorry." The words were staccato and brittle. "I'm the kid. She's my mother."

"You're right. She is your mother. But you're not much of kid anymore. You seem pretty grown up and independent." He smiled. "You're doing alright."

"Thanks." She appreciated the compliment, but it still didn't take away the fact that she was a disappointment to her mother.

"Well, let me settle this bill and get you back to whatever it was you were doing." He paused and then added cautiously. "How's the..."

"Fine." Her hand went to her flesh. Her lips compressed. The scar there was as fresh as the hurt she still had over the breakup. In fact, that surgery had come right on the heels of that breakup. The two things seemed pretty intertwined, and, while she knew they weren't, they still felt that way.

"That's good."

She nodded. She didn't want to talk about it. Not at all. It all still seemed so unfair and far too close to the surface. She didn't want to discuss it or even think about it either.

CHAPTER 5

An hour later she stood in front of the shop, debating the wisdom of just turning around and getting back in her car. Instead she took a deep breath and walked in. To her surprise, the shop was mostly empty and quiet. There was a hum of voices from behind the doors of the rooms but, unlike yesterday, the crowds were now gone and Hawk himself stood behind the counter.

He looked up and smiled broadly. "Hey, Joy!"

He knew her name! Her heart pounded and she drew slightly closer. She said, "I wanted to ask you something."

"Okay, shoot."

She swallowed hard. "Is it possible for me to get a tattoo?"

"Of course." His eyes raked her face and then his eyebrows came together slightly. "Do you want to go in there and discuss it?"

She nodded.

"Okay, come on in."

They headed into the room he'd tattooed Pixie in the night before. Her eyes wandered over the neat shelves and the pen and ink drawings on the walls while she tried to think of how to ask for what she wanted.

Which was just a tattoo.

Really.

Hawk sat down on his swivel chair, politely watching her. "Have you got anything in mind?"

She looked down. "I need to know...oh, you know what? This is silly. I can't get a tattoo." Humiliated and ashamed, she turned, but his hand caught her elbow and turned her back around.

"Are you afraid of the needle?"

She looked down and then back up. "No. I'm on blood thinners."

"That changes everything then, doesn't it?" His hand came out and he brushed a stray hair away from her face. "I mean for you. That's tough, and you're really young too."

His touch gave her shivers. "Yes. So I wondered...I wanted to know if you could paint something on my skin instead."

He looked surprised, but interested. "I've never tried that. I'm not even sure I have any paints that are good for skin. Wait, I do have some body paints. We all dressed up for Halloween and..." he turned and rummaged around in a drawer. "I think there's some brushes we didn't use too."

She knew her face was red; she could feel the burn of it on her cheeks and down her neck. "I-I don't want to put you through a lot of trouble."

He grinned at her. "You're not. This is cool. And different."

Her chest lifted and air filled her lungs. "You're a great artist."

He looked at the drawings hanging on the walls. "For some reason I love all kinds of canvas, but skin just draws me in. There's something so sensual and...dangerous, I suppose...about doing a tattoo even though we take all the precautions to be safe. But it's risky.

"People get their lover's names tattooed on them and they have no idea if that person's going to stay. They get dreams and hopes tattooed onto their skin and they know people can see that, and they have to acknowledge them when people ask about those tattoos."

She hadn't considered that. "I wonder what Pixie tells people when they see those 3-D tattoos of butterflies on her legs."

Hawk laughed. "That she's fae, of course."

Joy grinned. "She honestly believes she is, you know."

"I do know. It's part of why I like her so much. She's not like most people. Unique isn't a bad thing." He set the paints lined up in front of him. "So, what are we painting?"

"I don't know."

He searched her eyes and then he smiled. "I think I do. The question is, where do we paint it?"

She chewed on her lower lip and watched Hawk's green eyes drop to watch. "How long will it last?"

"A day or two."

"Could you do it on my back?"

"Absolutely. You'll have to take off the shirt and lie down."

Her face went scarlet and her hands shook. "Um..."

He turned his back. It was so sweetly chivalrous she wanted to cry. She quickly shed her shirt and she had a sudden and intense gratitude fill her. Thankfully she'd put on the pretty black lace bra that morning. The humor in that hit her, and she giggled as she got up on the table and flipped over on her belly.

Hawk spun, and his hand ran lightly on her back, making her shiver slightly. "You have great skin."

There was a slight tremor in his voice. She heard it. Or had she?

She bit her bottom lip and said, "So do you."

Oh.

My.

What the hell?

Had she just said?

She had. Tongue-tied and unsure what else to say, she lay still.

His hands moved along her skin and then he murmured, "Yeah, that'll work if I start from there."

The tip of the brush touched her back. The paint was cool but it warmed slowly, and she closed her eyes. It was erotic, maybe the most erotic thing she'd ever known, even more so than sex.

The paint slowly covered her skin. The brush moved in slow and sweeping strokes, then in fine and gentle brushes. Heat flushed along her lower body and her toes curled as he leaned close and low, his breath washing over her skin, sweeping across the wet paint to create a startling and tingling sensation that stiffened her nipples and made her eyes fly open wide.

"That's beautiful," he said softly, almost as if he were speaking to himself.

It was. Beautiful and sexy, and her skin burned beneath his touch and the sweep of the brush. Every cell came alive. Her nerve endings responded by sending little flares of heat, and her breath stuck in her throat.

Time ticked by, measured in the simple beat of her heart and the heavy pulse centered in the base of her throat, and the touch and withdrawal of his hands and the paint and the brush. Joy was lost in a haze of sensation and touch, and when he finally stopped she had to stop herself from blurting out for him to keep on painting her, to paint every inch of her skin.

"It has to dry for a little while," Hawk said. His low voice sent fresh electric-like tingles through her body. "I guess you're a captive audience for at least twenty minutes."

"That's okay." Her own voice was weak and slightly trembling.

Hawk didn't move, his body close the table. "You want to talk about it?"

"The ...um...paint tattoo?" She turned her head from the head rest and watched him as she slipped her forearm under her and lay the side of her face on her arm.

"No, why you're on blood thinners."

She closed her eyes and opened them again. She hated talking about it. People were always too kind or sympathetic. They always said the same things over and over too, but somehow she wanted to talk to him about it. That was odd, and yet she decided to just say it. "I had a slight birth defect in my heart. Nothing big or even unusual. I have an artificial valve now. I wasn't a good candidate for the less invasive surgeries, so they had to do an open heart procedure to place the valve. I wasn't near death, and I'm not dying."

"I see. That explains the ticking."

Usually that observance would have unnerved her, but he said it in such an off-handed way she had to laugh. "Yeah, it drives me crazy at night when it's really quiet. They say eventually I won't hear it much anymore."

"I imagine it'll just fade into the background eventually."

"And it makes for a great impression of the crocodile in Peter Pan."

His laughter was rich and full. It filled the room and warmed her inside.

She hesitated for a second then joined in. "I hate it when people assume I'm frail or weak or about to faint at any minute. In truth, I'm way better now than I was. I can't have too much salad or other so-called healthy food either. That's a bonus."

"People put way too much stock in thinking that being thin means you're healthy." Hawk made a noise that came close to a snort. "I've never understood it."

He wasn't into skinny? Rock on! "My mom and sisters are crazy-thin and I never was. They found out about my heart after I passed out on a treadmill when I was fifteen, and my mom seriously freaked out. Not because my heart was bad, because she was sure it was going to keep me from exercising."

Hawk's eyes grew wide. "That's awful! My mom used to smoke a cigarette with one hand and stir whatever she was cooking for dinner with the other. Drove me nuts. I was always sure there was going to be an ash somewhere in my food."

They both laughed again and Joy, still on her belly, asked, "Did you grow up here?"

"Yes. You?"

"Yeah, I grew up here too." She didn't say the rest of it. What was there to say? She'd grown up in Bel-Air. She'd gone to private schools and rubbed elbows with other rich kids. She generally didn't discuss that part of her life at all, not if she could help it. It led to way too many questions. Like who her parents were.

Hawk didn't press. Instead he said, "Since you can't get away, I figure I might as well take the chance and ask if you want to go to dinner."

She blinked. "I'm sorry?" She twisted her head to look at him and an immediate pain in her neck made her stop.

He walked closer, where she could see him. "I figured now would be the time to ask because you can't just run out screaming, "fuck you." Not without at least stopping to grab your shirt. That might give me enough time to convince you to go."

"Are you serious?" It suddenly occurred to her how silly she must look, gawking up at him.

He grinned. "Yes. Don't get me wrong, plenty of people have left here without putting on their shirts but I figure you aren't really the type."

She was torn between bewilderment and amusement. "Um, Hawk. I mean...um...I...guys don't ask me out a lot and...uh...I..."

"It's just dinner, Joy."

His words were kind. She had the eerie feeling that he was looking right through her, and seeing her. Really seeing her. It was disconcerting but somehow gratifying. It also left her searching for something to say. He was gorgeous. More than gorgeous. He was smoking-hot, and he probably had a lot of women who would love to go out with him coming into his shop every day. So why her? Why would he ask her out? "I know that. I just...I mean...I mean you could ask anyone out, so..."

Hawk pursed his lips and Joy had the sudden urge to lean over and kiss them. "You know what I can't figure out? How can someone who believes so passionately that all people need is a chance to believe in themselves not believe in herself?"

His words hit home. She shook her head. "I'm not a house."

"No, you definitely aren't. Sit up and I'll let you see your art."

She sat up slowly. All the same old fears came rolling in. Was that little stubborn pudge around her waist hanging over her waistband? Were her boobs about to explode out of her bra? Did he see the slight fullness of her belly? Should she sit up straight and suck it in, or just let him see her as she was?

Those never-ending litanies of self-doubt.

How she hated them.

His eyes went to the red ridge of scar. She looked down at it. Just another flaw. One of far too many. She couldn't go out with him. She couldn't. He would see all of it and wonder why he had ever asked her anyway in a minute.

He helped her up and over to a mirror. She managed to turn her head enough to see and her mouth dropped open.

There was a park, and small houses, clean streets, and a shining sun in the blue sky, all on her back.

Her dream, put right out there on her skin.

He had seen inside of her.

She swallowed hard. "Dinner would be nice."

Hawk smiled. "Oh, thank goodness you said yes. I was beginning to wonder if I'd forgotten deodorant. Or something worse!"

Joy doubled over laughing, all her worries forgotten for a moment. "No. You smell good to me. Really good."

"Oh, you noticed?" He held out her shirt and she took it.

He was kidding, but there was no way any female could miss his scent. She cleared her throat and blinked, trying to look normal, not like someone begging to get laid. "What do I owe you for the painting?"

His smile was wide. "Nothing. It's a slow day and it was interesting, and a challenge. I dug it."

She slipped her shirt on. The paint was dry now and she found she got a strange and warm satisfaction from knowing it was there but nobody else could see it.

It was hers, and hers alone.

And his.

Yes, it was his too.

She played with her last button after buttoning it up, "Um, what...er...dinner. When?"

"I work late tonight, so how about tomorrow if you're free?"

She nodded. "That sounds good. I could meet you here if that would work."

"It will. How about seven?"

"Seven it is."

Now that there was going to be a date, her awkwardness came back. "Should I give you my number?"

"Absolutely. And I'll give you mine."

They were exchanging numbers when there was a knock on the door. Hawk called out for the person knocking to enter. His receptionist stuck her head in and said, "I have Chloe Williams on the line. She won't talk to anyone but you. She says she's right outside in her car and wants to come in if you aren't busy."

Joy went pale. Chloe was an old acquaintance of sorts. She'd been a child star who'd briefly attended school with Joy, and as she'd grown up she'd worked with Joy's father from time to time. She lived in New York but spent a lot of time in L.A., and she knew Joy's face. That was all she needed, to run into someone who knew who she was and would tell Hawk before she was ready for him to know, if he didn't already.

"I'll let you get back to work," she said. She hurried out of the room and spotted a side exit. She took it and came out next to a tacky little store that she promptly ducked into. From inside it she had a good view of the street, and she waited until Chloe had gone by before heading to her car.

She got in and headed home. Her emotions swung from exultation to concern. Hawk had been on television, and according to Pixie he wasn't interested in any of it, but how could she know for sure? And if he was, had he asked her out because he, like Brian, thought she could help him with his career?

Or could he actually just genuinely like her?

She got home without managing to come to any conclusions, save one.

She really wanted to have dinner with him.

Inside her apartment she went through the listings for a few of the houses in the neighborhood she had targeted. Her smile got wider as she found a few she knew she could not only afford to buy but renovate as well. To make it even better, there were three being sold for a song. They were total teardowns, of course, but they were also side by side. The combined lots would be perfect for her green space plans.

Sitting back in her chair, she surveyed the listings again. This was a huge thing, and she knew it. She needed the cooperation of the neighborhood's residents, many of whom would be angry at the first sign of what they thought might be gentrification.

They'd seen blight and they'd seen gentrification. They knew neither was particularly good for them. She needed to actually talk to them and get them on board, and make them understand that she wasn't a developer interested in making their neighborhood a place they couldn't afford.

First things first, though. She had to actually buy the properties.

She had a trust fund that was enough to buy a small country if she wanted to. She'd never touched it even though she'd come into possession of the first half of it at twenty-one and the rest at twenty-five. She earned a good living, and lived well below her salary. She could afford the properties and the renovations, and not have to take much from her trust fund to do it.

It was risky, and she knew it but she was determined. This was the thing she'd been waiting for. The neighborhood was solidly blue-collar and middle-class. It wasn't the exact neighborhood she wanted to start working in, but if she could accomplish something there she might be met with a lot less suspicion on her next attempt.

She took a deep breath and picked up the phone to call a realtor she knew then paused. She wanted to call Hawk and tell him.

However, that was ridiculous. She barely knew him, and for all she knew his asking her out had been a spur of the moment thing and it might still fall through.

She called the realtor and then she called her banker. When her calls were finished, she stood and walked to the windows to look out on the tiny courtyard below. Her thoughts churned and raced.

She wanted to trust Hawk. Of course she did. He was smoking-hot, but even more attractive was that he was funny and intelligent. His touch had left her shivering and so turned on there'd been heat on her belly even after she'd gotten home.

Could he possibly really be interested in her?

She went to the bathroom and stared at her reflection. She was pretty enough, yes, but she wasn't the typical California girl, and she wasn't the actress-type at all.

Maybe that was appealing to him, though.

The taunts of her sisters and her classmates rang in her ears, and she groaned. She was too old to be letting the bullying she'd suffered as a child and teen keep messing with her head, and she knew it, but it was hard to shake.

She wanted to. Damn, she wanted to. She wanted to so badly but it was so hard. The scars had gone deep, and every time she thought that they were healed something came along to rip the scabs off and show her just how raw they still were.

Brian had been terrible for her. He'd been about the worst thing that could have happened to her, in fact; she knew that what had happened was his fault, and not hers, but no matter how much she understood that she couldn't seem to get past it either.

Well, she could start by going out with Hawk.

Yes, that was a good idea. So what if nothing came of it? So what if they just had dinner once and then never saw each other ever again? That would be okay. People went on one date all the time, and then didn't date that person again.

It was time to start reminding herself of the very things she'd said to Lily earlier that day. She was smart, and she was talented. She had a good job, and she had passion. It was time to start looking at herself like that instead of as someone who would never measure up to the expectations and hopes that her mother had had for her.

She paused. Was what her father had said to her at lunch even remotely true?

She wanted to believe it was, but she didn't underestimate her mother's ability to turn everything around and make it all about her and how hard she had it. She'd seen her do it far too often to buy into that just yet.

She could, however, accept that she was not the person her mother had imagined her to be, and that that was okay. She didn't need her mother's approval, not anymore. She'd wanted it desperately for far too long, and it had never come. It would probably never come, and it was high time she stopped trying to win that approval and just try to be the person she wanted to be, for herself. She wanted to reach her goals and see her dreams succeed, whether her mother ever understood or approved or not, and she felt a sudden sense of relief as she considered those things.

There'd been a heavy weight on her shoulders for a very long time, and now it was sliding away. It wasn't gone but it was slowly leaving.

It was about time too.

CHAPTER 6

Joy was utterly mystifying. Hawk had never had a woman agree to a date with him so reluctantly. He wasn't being cocky; it just had never happened before. Ironically, he had never wanted a girl to say yes more than at that moment.

He knew he probably should have let her go without pressing her to say yes. She'd probably go three feet and decide she'd made a terrible mistake and call him back tomorrow to say she'd changed her mind.

Or not call at all.

Hell, for all he knew, the number she'd given him was bogus. That thought made him want to call her and check. The whole situation stumped him. He had never really had a hard time getting women and he knew his bad-boy tattooed image hadn't hurt his past dating exploits, but he never had to wonder if a woman had given him a bogus number before.

He winced, remembering all the times he'd gotten numbers from women and not used them. Not because he had asked for them and changed his mind, but because he hadn't been interested in the woman who'd given them to him. Had they waiting by the phone, hoping he would call, and then felt the sting of disappointment when he hadn't?

Why hadn't he just said no thank you or told them he was taken or anything, but taken the number and forgotten about it?

Hawk believed strongly in Karma, and he had a bad feeling it was about to come around and kick him dead square in the ass.

There was something about Joy. Damn! He wanted to see inside her. Hell, he wanted to be inside her.

He took out his phone and stared at the screen. Her number was right there; it would be easy to press it, call her and then say he'd made a mistake, hit the wrong section of the screen or something. That was, if she answered. If it was a wrong number—no harm no foul. Nobody on the other end would have any idea who he was.

Unless they didn't answer and then called him back. Then he would answer, of course, and probably with his usual "Hawk from Fly High Tattoos, here," and then they would know.

Damn if he did, damned if he didn't. In a way.

Shaking his head at his own foolishness and sudden nerves, Hawk went out into the shop. There were a number of people milling around, looking at the walls, and the artists, who worked for what they charged for their work minus a fee for their work stations, were all trying to sell to the potential customers.

Hayley was talking to a heavily tatted and pierced young man who wanted to go up a few sizes on a piercing and Chris, his best artist next to himself, was busy chatting up a young man with a bright smile and an eager look in his eyes that Hawk knew all too well.

He spotted a guy slouching in the corner and headed for him. As soon as he approached, the dude perked up and said, "Hey there, you're Hawk."

"I am." He held out his hand and the guy shook it. Hawk nodded at the art book in the guy's hand. "You looking to get tatted?"

"I am, and I got a couple ideas of what I want."

Hawk, determined to stop worrying about whether or not Joy was going to call or show up for their date, tried to listen and focus on the guy's mediocre drawings, but all he could think about was Joy's skin under his fingers and the way she'd gone so soft and pliant beneath him as he worked on her delicious back.

Damn it.

The woman had him totally enthralled.

CHAPTER 7

The next day, Joy couldn't stop the tremors running through her body. She blamed it on nervousness, refusing to admit it might be excitement. Hawk seemed to have the ability to make her blood run hot. No! It wasn't him. Her body's reaction had to deal with the men in her past and her inability to trust them.

She'd been afraid to call Hawk; sure he would tell her that he had changed his mind. Maybe he would say it nicely, like he had to work longer than he thought or that he was tired from working. Or suddenly he would remember he had something else to do.

"You're being ridiculous," she muttered to herself. She checked her phone for the hundredth time to see no message to cancel dinner. She walked over to the full-length mirror and gave herself a critical stare. "Joy," she told her reflection, "the man asked *you* to dinner." She turned halfway and glanced at the stunning painting on her back. She'd been careful in the shower, using cold water; afraid hot would erase it sooner. It had stayed on, almost near perfectly. *Just like the artist*, she thought. She stood in a black lace bra and matching panties. They were an expensive purchase and she'd bought them on a whim.

She leaned over and grabbed her phone off her bed and found Hawk's number in her contacts. She hit call and tried to ignore the sudden racing of her hot. *Was it hot in here?* She fanned herself with her free hand.

When he picked up she spoke quickly, "I just wanted to make sure we were still on. I mean, if you've something else to do that's okay, I just didn't want to drive down and find out after I'd driven." Her breath came way too fast, making whooshing sounds through the phone speaker. She wondered if she were about to hyperventilate or something.

Hawk's husky, low voice came through, causing her to catch her breath and suddenly hold it in, "We're still on. I've zero intention of calling it off."

She took a quick pained gasp. "Good. Um...what should I wear?"

"Come again?"

She blushed and turned from the mirror so she couldn't see her own face. "I was just wondering if I should dress up or if we're going casual. If I need to wear a dress, or a skirt, or maybe jeans. Are we going to be eating meat? Or do I need to take my lobster bib?" She knew she was babbling and sounding like an idiot. She didn't even own a freakin' lobster bib! Fuck!

His sexy chuckle teased her ear. "I tell you what, you show up in whatever you're wearing right now."

She swung around, her eyes huge as she stared at her near-naked self. "I-I can't," she managed.

"Why not?"

"I'm uh, just in my, uh, undergarments." She sounded like a slut trying to hit on him. Her hand covered her face as she shook her head. Did she hear his breath catch? "Where are we going? I'll figure something out."

"How about you wear what you want and we'll go out based on what you wear? Is that fair?"

It was. It was also dangerous, but spontaneous and exciting too. She wasn't used to someone who played things out as they came. Brian had been as structured and hemmed in as an old man, and the few guys she had dated before that were all about the same.

They always had a plan, and Hawk seemed willing to just go with the flow. It was new, and it was oddly thrilling.

"Okay," she said. "That sounds good. I'll see you at seven."

She hung up and did a happy little dance across her bedroom. Her phone rang again and her heart sank, thinking it would be her mother, or stepsister. She saw Pixie's number on the screen and quickly flicked it on.

Before she could say hello, Pixie groaned, "Oh hot hell! I learned to crush grapes. With my feet. They're fucking purple. It's gross. I'll never drink wine again as long as I live."

"I'm going on a date with Hawk." The words spilled out of her before she could stop them.

Pixie let out a triumphant whoop. "You go girl! Seriously?"

"Yup." She grinned feeling proud.

"I told ya so! Don't forget to call me after you're done. Not like *right* after. You better be in bed right after and not alone either. Let those artist hands do some magic to your body."

"Pixie!"

Pixie howled laughter and hung up. Joy headed into her closet to try to find something to wear.

An hour later, her bedroom literally destroyed, she did a full circle and scowled at the mess. Heaps of discarded clothes were everywhere. Her hair had been put into a braid, taken down, slicked back into a twist, taken out. Curled. Brushed out. Braided again and, in a final desperate act, she added a little jeweled headband to it and hoped Hawk wouldn't notice that she'd managed to frizz out her ends and snarl the little tendrils of hair that had escaped the braid.

She'd changed clothes so many times she really had no idea if the outfit she was wearing even matched anymore. She hoped it looked okay. She wore a long blue silk blouse with a wide belt, long black leggings tucked into half-boots, and carried a slim black purse.

She took several long breaths, considered changing again, changed her mind, and headed into the kitchen. She'd read that the best way not to look like she was an overly-eater eager on a date was to have a snack before she went. She was determined to do that but when she opened her refrigerator all she found was some leftover Chinese that had somehow managed to sprout hair that had grown to the point that it hung over the sides of the carton, a few wilted looking pre-packed salads, and a suspiciously dark apple.

She groaned and rummaged in the cabinets looking for chips or a cookie, but Pixie's love of junk food extended to vegan things she was sure were going to be horrible and when she tried a carob-and-fig bar, she was proven right.

Time had gotten away from her and she had to hurry. Deciding to say to hell with the snack-first option, she dashed out the door, into the elevator to the parking garage, where her courage came close to failing her.

It somehow didn't, though, and she got in her car and drove straight to the shop, her hands clutching the steering wheel tight.

Why did she want to impress this particular guy so badly?

CHAPTER 8

Hawk looked up from a drawing book a hopeful artist had brought, a sampling of his work, and his heart nearly stopped. Joy stood framed in the doorway, the dying sun behind her back lighting up her hair. She looked nervous enough to bolt at any minute too.

"Tell you what, dude," he said to the guy sitting on the couch by him. "You come in tomorrow and we'll give you a road test and see."

The man, Hawk was pretty sure his name was Cliff, nodded vigorously and said, "Yeah sure. What time you want me here?"

Hawk looked back at Joy. She came a little further into the shop but her expression hadn't changed a bit. "Oh, say noon. You'll be inking me, by the way, so bring your A-game."

"Dude, I thought you were going to give me something that would intimidate me." He laughed.

Hawk liked him. He was about twenty-five or six, cocky as all hell, and he had the good looks that would draw female customers. "In that case, you can ink-up our crash test dummy."

"You got a crash test dummy?"

"Yeah, and her name is Pixie."

Joy spoke up, drawing the guys' attention. "Pixie's in Napa, making wine with her feet. She says it's gross."

Cliff turned to look at Joy and instantly jealousy smote Hawk. That feeling was so alien he didn't even know how to register it. He wanted to shout, 'Hands-off! She's mine.'

Cliff shot her a handsome smile. "When's she coming back?"

Joy shrugged. "I can call her and ask. Hold on. Wait. Does she know you use her as a crash test dummy?"

Hawk chuckled, "Yeah it's why she gets those 3-D tats from me free."

"And she's okay with it?" Joy still didn't look convinced.

Hawk smiled. Man, she was sexy. "It was her idea, actually."

Joy rolled her eyes jokingly. "In that case, let me give her a shout." She called Pixie, who announced she was coming back the next day and could come into the shop the day after.

Cliff clapped his hands and rubbed them together. "I can come in then."

He and Hawk shook on it and Cliff left.

Hawk turned his full attention to the beauty standing in front of him. "You look great."

Her smile was shy. "I...um, I messed up my hair a little." Her face went red. It was endearing, that blush, but it also made him wonder if she got that same red flush when she was close to orgasm. His jeans tightened and he shifted, glad he was still behind the counter. "Do you like the Pier?"

"I love it." Her eyes fastened to his face. "Especially the Ferris Wheel."

"Me too. You want to go there?"

"I'd love to."

He waited a moment to give his jeans time to loosen, and then moved around to the other side of the counter. His night manager, Rob, was already in the shop and everything was set up to go for the evening, so he walked out without looking back. "I brought my car instead of the bike, so we can take my car if you'd like."

She fiddled with her keys. That vulnerability and fear called to him. She'd been hurt, and it showed. He wanted to find the man who'd done that to her and throttle him. "That's fine."

She walked beside him. Her perfume, a light floral scent, drifted to his nose. Her hair gave off the scent of lilacs and what smelled like jasmine. Her smooth skin was so satiny in appearance he wanted to touch it, and he had to wrack his brain to think of something to say that wouldn't make him sound like a lecher.

They stopped at his black Mustang, and he held her door for her.

She murmured, "Thank you," and then reached over and opened his, a move that impressed him.

He pulled out of his parking spot and headed toward the water. They started to talk, and to his relief they quickly discovered that they had a lot in common.

They had a shared love of Thai food, the beach, football—and she was serious fan who knew her team's stats and the players as well as he did—and they both loved rock music, action movies, and the color green. She pushed that, saying his eyes were her favorite color. He loved it.

By the time they reached the pier, they were laughing and talking like old friends and Hawk knew he wanted her. Badly. Not just for a night either. He knew she was the kind of woman he would want for a very long time. "Ferris wheel first, or food?"

"Ferris wheel." She smiled. "I'd rather have fun first. That is, unless you'd rather eat first."

He grinned, wanting to kiss her. "Oh, I hear a challenge there. Let's ride, bab—Joy."

She laughed as they wound their way down to the Ferris wheel and bought the tickets to ride it and a few other things. They climbed into a car and zoomed upward into the darkening sky. The lights twinkled all around them and the bucket rocked gently. Joy clutched the bar and leaned way over, craning to see the ground below.

"My dad used to sneak me out here," she said.

He watched her, one eyebrow raised. "Your mom didn't approve?"

"Oh, hell no! Nothing about the pier was good in her book. Junk food, rides that might kill you, crowds of..." her mouth snapped shut.

Hawk wondered what it was she'd been about to say, but he didn't press. "My dad brought us kids here too. He used to pretend he hated it but he was always the first one out of the car."

She leaned closer, her perfume making him crazy. "You have brothers and sisters?"

"Three brothers. One sister." Two brothers now, but he always said three anyway. "How about you?"

"I'm an only child of sorts. I have three half-sisters and one half-brother, though." She held her hands out and let the lights shine through the gaps in her fingers and the smile on her face was almost heartbreakingly innocent.

He wanted to kiss her.

Badly.

He wanted to lean across the car and capture her lips with his. Kiss her in the high and rocking seat, kiss her while the mildly salt-tinged air passed over their faces and bodies. It had taken all of his self-control not to kiss her the day before while she'd been in the shop, and he was having trouble resisting that urge just then.

He tilted his head toward her but the car began its descent, lurching so hard she was thrown away from him and against the other side of the car. "Shit! Are you okay?"

She nodded and giggled. "Yeah, I'm good. Happens all the time."

"I should have remembered and took that side."

The car finished its descent and they got off. He wished he hadn't spent so much time thinking about kissing her. It would have been romantic. Not high school romantic, but the kind of kiss that he would remember how it felt and that exact moment they were up there romantic. *Idiot*, he scolded himself. He took her hand instead and helped her out.

She let her hand stay in his. "Carousel?"

"Of course. We're hitting all the rides. If you can take it, that is." He grinned down at her and swallowed. If she stopped walking, he was going to kiss her right here. Press his lips against her soft sweet pink ones and slip his tongue—

She jerked his hand and laughed. "What're you waiting for?"

CHAPTER 9

Joy knew the carousel was a bit of silliness, but she loved the creaking old thing. She and Hawk got on and took a low seat. They sat close together, their bodies touching, and she let herself lean closer to him. He wore a fantastic-smelling cologne and it made her want to put her face in his neck and sniff it, lick it, and kiss it.

His arm came up and draped over her shoulder. The heat and weight of it felt perfect and she snuggled backward to get closer. Just the side of his arm rested against the back of her bare neck and little shivers traced up and down her spine. Her toes curled inside her shoes when the ride took off and they slid closer to each other, their hips and thighs colliding. The lights and music were festive and bright, and she found herself laughing for no reason at all.

"I'm not really a nut-job," she shouted over the music of the ride. "Honest."

Hawk smiled as the ride continued. "If I thought you were a loon, I'd have left you on the Ferris Wheel with a clown."

They got off the ride and headed for the exit gate, but before they got there he turned to her. Her heart beat so fast up against her rib cage she actually looked down to make sure it was still inside her chest and hadn't jumped right out of it.

His finger tipped her chin back. His mouth came down on hers, and she tasted spearmint and mouthwash. His lips were firm but soft and she closed her eyes and leaned against him, her hands going to his shoulders.

His tongue slid into her mouth, and she let herself respond. The kiss was soft and slow but it intensified quickly and she rubbed against him, forgetting completely about the crowds streaming around them.

Someone yelled, "Get a room!"

They broke apart with a laugh.

Joy stood dazed, her lips slightly bruised from the fierceness of the kiss. Her breath came a little too quickly and she murmured, "Well...um...that was nice."

"Damn nice," Hawk said with a grin. "How about we get something to eat? I'm scared I'm going to start trying to bite you." He took her hand and led her toward a restaurant where people sat outside at tables, watching the stars and the Ferris wheel spinning above them.

They sat and ordered fries, burgers, and onion rings. As they waited for their food to come, Joy dug up her courage and forced herself to look into his beautiful green eyes. "I have a question for you."

"Shoot!"

"I don't know why you asked me out. Why did you?"

Hawk, sipping his beer, lifted an eyebrow. "You don't?"

She shook her head. "No, I don't."

He set the beer down and leaned across the table. "Because I think you're gorgeous; because you're nice, and kind, and you have a passion for something bigger than being an actress or making it in in the shit industry that's all around us. It really appeals to me."

She was pleased and embarrassed at the same time. Her? Gorgeous? "Well, I don't know about all that, but I really don't care for the shit industry either." She took a small sip from her beer and continued to stare at him. "If you hate it, why did you do that show?"

He sighed and leaned back. "Well, I guess I figured I needed the exposure. I worked at a lot of shops as an intern so I could learn as much as I could before I set up my own. I had a good client and regular customer base, but rents in L.A. are seriously crazy, and I'm not foolish enough to think I didn't need some sort of boost. When the offer presented itself, I couldn't see a solid reason to say no." He took a long swallow of his beer. "What I didn't know was how crazy and intrusive it would be."

"I can imagine."

Hawk pressed his lips tight. "No, you really can't. Or...I don't know...have you ever been on reality television?"

"Hell no! I don't even like my picture taken." She played with the cheap napkin under her bottle, "Yeah, you're right. I probably can't imagine." She could more than imagine, if the truth were told. She knew exactly how much the cameras intruded in Lily's private spaces, and just how little privacy she really had. She couldn't exactly say that though.

Hawk sighed. "It was awful. I told them they could only be in the shop, and the next thing I knew they were following me out at night, and trying to bargain their way into my home. They were insistent that if I wanted to keep my privacy I should never have done the show. I know they do the same thing to everyone, but I didn't invite them into my house; I invited them into my shop."

"There's a fine line between celebrity and a fishbowl. Sometimes there's no line. I couldn't do it. I like my privacy. I need it, in fact."

Hawk smiled. "Me too. I'm not a serial killer or anything, I promise! But I work around people all day. I'm always busy, and when I'm done I don't like to go hang out at clubs and party. I did when I was younger, like my early twenties. But as I get older, I have more responsibilities and they keep me from doing the things I used to do. I won't say I mind, because I don't. I was wild early on and I got my feet back under me early too. I like my life, and I don't want to have to explain it to the world at large, so I didn't want people examining it."

She stared at him. He had just said everything she had felt for so long. She couldn't say that either, not without telling him why she knew what he meant so she said, "I'm a real introvert. I like...not being alone like a hermit, which is what people think I mean when I say that. I mean, I love going out, but I hate crowded clubs. Not just because it's too many people but because...well, I always end up standing on the curb watching the 'hot' girls go by and get in."

The waiter brought their food and he helped set it on the table. When the waiter left, Hawk continued, "That's something else I hate about L.A., and the world in general. That whole being unrealistically thin is what makes women attractive thing."

She stared at him for a long moment, the aroma of deep fried food and grilled hamburgers wetting her palate, but the look in his eyes is was caught her more. "Hawk, you do know you don't have to say that, don't you? I mean, I know what my size is."

His eyes flashed. He leaned forward and stole an onion ring from her plate, "Let me tell you something. If I say something, I mean it. I hate lies, and I hate people who use them. I don't lie. I also really don't find women who starve themselves to twenty pounds below their healthy weight attractive, especially if they do it in the hopes of landing a part or to be what society deems as pretty. I think it's fucking stupid. My piercer, Hayley, she's getting incredibly close to fainting from starvation. If it keeps up, I'm going to have to fire her. Not because she wants to be thin no matter what, but because her not eating is effecting her ability to think and react, and eventually it's going to cause a serious injury at my shop. Plus, it's not sexy." He popped the onion ring into his mouth and pointed at her. "This is sexy." He covered his mouth full of food and spoke behind it. "Probably doesn't sound that way coming from a guy stuffing his face with stinkin' onion." He finished his bite and took a quick swig of his beer to wash it down. "This is the truth: I love curves on a woman. I like hips I can wrap my hands around. I love the feel of flesh over bones, and the way bodies move. I love the way it looks, not leaving the bones all exposed, and I fucking love the fact that you're curvy and gorgeous and strong. I love the way you look. It's fucking sexy as all hell."

Her mouth fell open. She'd dated guys who'd sworn her weight wasn't a problem, but she'd never had one tell her they liked her for it. Mostly they said they didn't notice it. And the truth was—they had. They had and she'd been so grateful to be asked out she had just let that go, instead of examining the inherent problem with that statement.

If they didn't see her size, then they didn't see her. Or, worse, they did see it and they pretended they didn't. They didn't want to see it. They didn't like it, much less think it was, as Hawk had said, sexy as hell.

Her entire body burned with a rising tide of passion. Hawk was nothing like anyone she'd ever met, and she knew that was part of. Those arms of his, those strong and colorful arms with the beautiful pictures tattooed all over them, were part of it. That air of danger that hung all around him was part of it too.

Everything about him made her crazy with wanting.

She smiled shyly, hoping her crazy attraction for him wasn't as obvious as she felt it was. "I don't even know what to say to that, but thank you." Her voice dropped to a lower tone. "I...I think you're sexy as hell too and I wish, I really do, that I had a little more experience with...well, with dating, and especially dating men who look like you, but I don't."

Hawk chuckled. "Men like me? There's nothing special about me." He ran his fingers through his hair, the tattoo sleeve of his right arm beautiful against the pier lights. He was beyond handsome and he had no idea? "How about this? How about we just have some fun tonight? I'm just a guy, you're just a girl. No past, no pressure, just now."

Her pulse sped up again, and she began to wonder if she was going to wear out her new heart valve right there on their first date. "It's a deal." She wondered if hopping over the table and jumping him there in the restaurant would be out of the question. She grinned. *Not in my imagination.*

CHAPTER 10

Joy did have fun. It wasn't something she did often, as she was usually too guarded with people. She'd gotten so used to waiting for the other shoe to drop, for someone to ask her for something, that she had never been able to just relax and be herself with anyone.

It came to her as they walked along the pier and then the beach that she had never even really relaxed around her ex, Brian. She'd known deep down that he was just biding his time. She hadn't even been stricken the first time he had asked her for something, because she'd been expecting it. She pushed her thoughts of him out of her head and pretended to throw him in the ocean with the little stone she tried skipping on top of the water.

Hawk and she were in the car headed back to the shop when Joy realized she didn't want the night to end. Just fun, right? No, pressure, right? She had a little boldness in her after all. "Would you like to see my place?"

Hawk's hand rested lightly on her knee, his thumb tapping lightly to the tune playing softly on the radio. "I'd love to."

Little sparks flew between them. She wanted to kiss him again, even though he was driving. She wanted to do something sexy and brazen, like give him a blowjob right then, but she was too afraid he'd think she was easy, or he'd crash the car, or worse, they'd get stopped by the cops. All her thoughts ended in utter embarrassment.

It made her laugh inwardly, but by the time they got her apartment she had a real concern. She'd left her bedroom a total mess!

They got in the door and she offered, "Do you want a drink or..."

He caught her in a tight embrace. His arms went around her and she melted against him, rubbing herself against his body, feeling every lean muscle and hard bone beneath his clothes. It was more intoxicating than any drink.

The kiss grew as they shuffled toward her bedroom. She tore her mouth away from his and mumbled, "Oh shit! I couldn't figure out what to wear..."

Hawk stepped inside and kicked a frilly blue bra and a blouse out from under his feet, seized her in his arms, and mumbled as his lips found her neck, "Well, you made the right choice."

They landed on her bed in the middle of a pile of clothes. She got her arm tangled up in a thong and he plucked it off, gave it a long look, and then threw it over his shoulder. They rolled past a strewn stack of blouses and a slip and then his hands were on her body, stripping off her clothes with practiced ease.

The darkness of the room half hid her, and she grew brazen because of it. She explored his body as she bared it, her hands touching every sleek angle and running down his soft and taut skin. His piercing green eyes met hers, and he smiled. She lay in only her bra and panties; he in just boxer-briefs. "I'm not sure..." His gaze travelled down the length of her body and then slowly back up. He swallowed.

She drew strength out of his struggling as he tried to go slowly and ask. She wanted him, but he wanted her just as badly. She shook her head, as if trying to clear it, but only prolonging his sweet agony a few minutes longer.

That's a damn sexy bra." He traced a finger over the soft flesh of her breast, pressing against the top of it, and her breath quickened as he trailed down her stomach and along the thin line of her panties.

She slipped her hand along the back of his hair and tugged gently. "Get over here." She lifted her head to brush her lips against his.

Hawk needed no further encouragement. He crushed his lips against hers, his tongue forcing itself into her mouth. Heat stirred inside of her and sent tingling sensations deep into her belly. She could feel herself grow wet and he grew harder against the inside of her thigh.

She reached for the elastic on the top of boxers and pulled them down. "You are incredibly hot," she whispered, and sucked in a sharp breath as he lifted his hips and pulled his boxer-briefs to his ankles in one motion and then shook them off. Joy ran her fingernails down his muscular spine and over his tight glutes.

He groaned deep in his throat as his hips rotated with a mind of their own. He lay on top of her, one elbow holding him up above her and the other hand cupped her breast hungrily. He found the front clip of her bra and popped it open, freeing her heavy breasts. His mouth fell onto her nipple and he began sucking, and then let his tongue twirl around the hardening bud.

Joy couldn't think straight as her head fell back onto the pile of clothes, creating a makeshift pillow.

"Wow," he murmured, his breath hot against her skin. "You're beautiful." His hand stroked her other breast while his mouth continued to suck on one. Both nipples grew hard at his touch.

Joy could feel him smile against her breast as he moved and shifted. His thumbs hooked onto the thin lace at the top of her black lace panties. He left a trail of blazing hot kisses down her stomach, and then over the lace and down against the one spot on her body begging to be touched.

She sighed and it turned into a moan when Hawk's finger slipped inside her panties and rubbed her sensitive folds.

"Can I take these off?" he whispered.

"Please do."

In one pull, he had them off and his mouth captured where his finger had just been. His tongue bathed her. Wetness poured from her inner walls and coated his tongue. Her fingers tangled in his hair and her hips bucked upward sharply. His breath washed over the skin of her inner thighs, heat rolled through her, and she cried out, teetering on the edge of release. She came, her body exploding in ripples of pleasure over and over.

Hawk moved over top of her when her body slowly calmed. He muttered, "Shit. No condom."

"The other bathroom," she gasped. "Pixie keeps enough for a fleet. She hands them out to people..." She gasped as he moved off of her and a wave of cool air drifted over her heated body.

He got up and practically ran from the room, coming back with a strip of condoms dangling from one hand. He got one on and then joined her on the bed again.

He entered her slowly, his fingers finding that hard, pounding nub of flesh at the top of her hood again. Sensation spiked, and her body shuddered wildly beneath his thrusting body. He moved quickly, his large member sliding with precision and determination.

Joy came again, hard. Her body strained as she grunted under him. Her nails raked along his back and he went rigid as he found his orgasm too. His weight bore down on her, pressing her deeper into the mattress, and she sighed contentedly.

He chuckled after he dropped down beside her, trying to catch his breath. "I swear I just felt like a teenage kid again there for a minute. I guess that wasn't as suave as I had planned it to be." His chest rumbled with laughter against hers.

She giggled. "I have to admit I thought I would have time to clean my room. I'm honestly neat and organized. Most of the time."

"Oh. Was your plan to distract me with a beverage?"

"Yes." She said it so promptly that he snorted.

He rolled away long enough to remove the condom and then discard it in the wastebasket near her bed. He cuddled her close, and his finger went to her scar. He traced it gently. She shied away at first but then she relaxed and let it him.

He lifted his head and kissed it lightly. "Did it hurt?"

"Like hell."

He shifted slightly. "Doe sit still hurt?"

"No. The swelling's gone now, but that was what was really sore. It's still weird. I mean, having had it done and all."

"I would be scared shitless if it happened to me."

"I was terrified. I mean, I knew it was okay. I would be okay. It was just a stupid birth defect. My dad had it too, and he had to have surgery too, but he was in his fifties before he got his. The same year I was born, in fact. So I knew I was young, and that it was better to do it early, but it was still pretty scary."

"I bet. And I thought I was tough."

She stared at the ceiling, part of her wondering why she was telling him when she'd never told anyone else before. "The scariest thing was going in the hospital. That and the damn skydiving trip I went on right before."

Hawk sat up and looked at her. "What?"

"I figured if I was going to die I'd better cram as much experience into my life as I could get first."

"You went skydiving?"

"Yes."

"Are you nuts?"

She laughed, "I think I was, yes."

"I have to admit it I'm not, no way in hell, ever, jumping out of a plane."

"Oh, I said that too, but then I did."

He peered into her face. "Would you do it again?"

"Not a chance."

His hand stayed on her hip. It felt right there, and she rested her head on his shoulder. She asked, "So, how did you become a tattoo artist?" She couldn't believe they were lying on top of a pile of clothes, completely naked.

"When I was about ten, this guy moved in next door to us. He had these fucking amazing tattoos he'd gotten in Bangkok, all over his arms and chest. It was incredible and he had a story for each little part of it. How he'd gotten it, and what it meant to him. He literally wore his heart and his life on his sleeves, his tattoo sleeves, and it hit me then that it wasn't just art he had; it was his life." Hawk's voice grew thick with excitement and feeling. "I fell in love with the idea that people could wear it all out in the open, and I guess I also had this whole sort of guy-crush on his sleeves, and his bike. Anyway he had a friend, real guitar-string tattooist..."

She asked, "A what?"

He chuckled. "Lots of people get these tattoos done in jail, with ink made out of whatever. Burned funny papers and a little shank or a homemade tat gun, or they go to the guys they know in the neighborhood who have a gun, but don't buy fresh needles because they're expensive. They buy their ink at hobby stores and run guitar strings through their guns. It works."

"Damn! Seriously?"

He nodded, she could feel it on the pillow beside her. "Yeah, I say that now, but back then I'd sit for hours watching this guy tat in my neighbor's garage. I mean, it was funky. Oil and trash everywhere, dimly-lit, and everyone drinking or smoking weed. My neighbor wouldn't let him touch me and, in fact, he took me aside and told me why getting that kind of tattoo was stupid."

"Because you couldn't figure that out fast enough on your own?"

"Because I was a kid and all I saw were these people getting tattoos in what, to me, was the coolest way ever. I started drawing little things when I was about five and I had a little paint kit. I started selling my drawings to the folks who would go over there on tat days, and before long I realized that people were wearing stuff I dreamed up. And that they would always wear it."

She traced her hand over the tattoos on his forearm. "I never thought about it like that. I mean, that it comes from someone who draws it. I always just thought of what it meant to the people who got them. Or maybe I just wondered why people got them, but never really understood the whole thing really. I get it now, though. You fell in love with it, grew passionate about it, and then decided to do it for a living?"

Hawk chuckled. "I don't know if I did that. I think I thought it was cool to know those guys, and to be making money. I liked it, but I think I knew even then that wasn't how I wanted to tattoo. Because I had Bill, my neighbor, and those incredible sleeves that made everything his buddy did look cheap and funky." He shifted slightly and added, "Then when I was about fourteen or so, Bill moved on. My dad lost yet another job and my mom had to work longer hours. I wanted to help her out so I started riding my bike a few miles away, to this tattoo shop. I figured I could sell some drawings there."

He paused, and Joy's heart froze for a moment. He didn't have a fairytale story, and she had a feeling he didn't share this very often.

"The guy threw me out at least a dozen times before he would even look at my book. Then he decided to buy a few things. He sat me down and talked to me, and said come back when I was old enough to shave."

"Did you go back?"

Hawk nodded. "As soon as I got hair in my armpits I went back. He gave me an ink gun and told me if he caught me running string or doing back door tattoos through it, he'd kill me. I had to use it to practice on these damn little pieces of fruit. Tomatoes and melons and shit. Then take it back to him and show him what I had done. He said anyone who could tattoo that could intern under him. Took me two fucking years to get him to let me have a needle and a year after that to get ink."

She was impressed. "*That* is dedication."

He nodded. "I practiced my first tats on myself. See?"

He held out his arm and she looked at where his finger pointed. In the intricate designs on his arms she saw small hearts and stars, a delicate woman's face. She let her fingers wander over those pieces of his history and heart, and her heart swelled slightly. "They're beautiful."

"Thank you."

"Is it a problem that I can't get one?" It was a silly question, but she asked anyway.

He lifted her chin so she could look him in the eyes. "No. I would never endanger anyone, Joy. I can't remodel a house, and I hope that wouldn't count against me with you."

"Of course not," she protested.

"Then why would you not being able to have a tat bother me?"

It seemed silly when he put it that way. "I do think those butterflies you are doing on Pixie's legs are beautiful. When I first saw them I thought they were real. It looks like...when she walks, it looks like they are about to take flight or are flying all around her." A hard lump filled her throat. "It must be amazing to have that kind of beauty on your skin."

"I'll paint whatever you want on your skin." His words were warm and soft.

"Thank you." She paused and asked, "Do you just want to take me back to get my car in the morning or...or do you want to stay the night?"

"Do you want me to stay?"

She nodded. "Yes, but won't people notice if you wear the same clothes to work?"

"I can buy fresh clothes next door." His hand moved slowly up and down her body, sending little throbs of aching desire into her.

She closed her eyes to enjoy the touch. She wanted him to make love to her again, but she was sleepy too. She knew she didn't want him to leave.

Before she realized how, the morning sun was bright when she opened her eyes again.

CHAPTER 11

Pixie asked, "So tell me, did you?"

Joy gave her a long stare. "That's not polite to ask, you know."

"You did!" Pixie jumped up and down and then sat in a chair, her slight body showing interest with every line. "Do you like him? Are you going out again?"

Joy giggled, unable to stop the giddy feelings whenever she thought, or talked, about Hawk. "We are. Tomorrow night. After he watches that guy tattoo you. I can't believe you're going to do that."

"Hawk wouldn't even give him a shot if he didn't have good portfolio." Pixie said.

"Pixie's insane," Caligula stated from his cage.

Joy glanced at the cage and nodded knowingly at Caligula. "The bird knows."

Pixie grinned and said, "This calls for a celebration. Ice cream and cookies."

"No thanks. You eat that weird soy ice cream."

"I like coconut milk ice cream." Pixie pouted, clearing disappointed.

"Okay, well, I like real ice cream." Joy smiled and added, "And I have a meeting. So, raincheck?"

"A meeting?"

"With my client. For the house out in Malibu. Which I'm going to be late for if I don't get going."

Pixie grabbed Joy's hand as she slipped out of the booth. "Okay, raincheck, but I'm not forgetting this."

"I know you won't." Joy stood and headed for the door then stopped. "Are you okay?"

Pixie smiled. "Yeah, why?"

Joy said, "Well it's just that...it's just that you're always preaching to me about getting back out there and all, but you haven't dated either, not since..."

"Oh, don't say it. I know." Pixie fluttered her hands at Joy and said, "I'll get around to falling in love again. The difference between us is that without a hard push you'd hide from it forever. I'm not hiding. I'm just being prudent."

"And that's not hiding?"

"No."

Joy laughed, "Duly noted." She headed out. As she drove toward the site of the home she was designing for her client, she let her mind go to Hawk. He was wonderful, and she knew she could fall in love with him very easily if she let herself... except there was a giant reason why she had to be careful.

Her last name, and all that it entailed.

That thought stayed with her the next day as she watched the new tattoo artist, Cliff, carefully work on a small section of Pixie's back. She'd seen the look on Pixie's face when she saw him, and knew that Pixie was immediately interested. Joy hid her smile while she wondered if the mewling little sounds Pixie was making were because the needle and his hands felt similar to the way it had felt when Hawk had painted her body. Had she made the same noises?

She was disappointed that her paint tattoo had entirely washed away already. It had been so pretty she had hated to see it go, but had to admit she didn't miss the way it stained her clothes after a shower.

Hawk looked over the tiny little heart and dagger Pixie had asked for, a highly-detailed thing, and nodded briskly. "Cool.

Okay, I got one room. If you want it, it's yours. Let's go in the office and talk."

They left and Joy waited for Pixie to dress.

When she finished putting her shirt on, Pixie grinned. "Damn, he's hot."

"Which one?"

Pixie rolled her eyes. "Cliff."

"Oh, the guy who tattooed you?"

"No, his twin brother. Yeah, him." Pixie laughed and lifted her shirt to get a better view of her new tattoo. "Good with his hands as well."

"He's handsome, yeah, but he has those big holes in his ears and that's weird."

Pixie lifted an eyebrow and chuckled. "To each their own I guess."

Hawk came back in. "You ready?"

"Definitely!" She smiled and pointed to his ear. "See Pixie, no dangly bits or rings. Just cute, little perfectly-shaped ears. The way they're supposed to be."

Pixie laughed. "Hawk, can you get her out of here?"

He grinned. "Gladly."

Joy bade Pixie goodbye, handed over her car keys so Pixie could get home, and walked to Hawk's sleek black sports car with him. "Where are we going today?"

"I figured since you like art so much we'd go to the Getty."

She smiled. "I love the Getty."

They got in and Hawk put one hand on her knee. The bright California sunshine beamed down on them. Desire burned through her body at the light touch, and her nipples stiffened, pushing against the fabric of her thin blouse and the pretty bra she wore beneath it.

Hawk made her feel like a woman. He made her feel sensual and wanted. He made her body respond simply because she knew he saw her as a woman with a body he loved to touch, and not a body he could find some pleasure in despite its flaws. Hawk didn't see her as being flawed, and that made her so hot she could barely breathe at all around him.

They did go to the Getty. She tried to enjoy it but all she wanted to do was strip away his clothing and touch him, run her fingers up and down his bare skin and feel his body on hers. She wanted his thick, hot cock inside her, deep, and she wanted to feel his ass moving below her fingertips as he went deeper and deeper into her body.

After dinner Hawk asked if she wanted to go to a show or see his place. She answered 'your house' so fast she was sure he knew exactly how turned on she was.

He drove above the speed limit and they got to his house quickly, but it wasn't fast enough. Joy leaned over the seat and kissed him before the car was in park. He groaned and finally pulled away when the windows started to fog. They started kissing again in the driveway, and by the time they got inside they were both partially undressed.

Joy's hands found the buttons on his shirt and then his jeans. She filled her palm with his hardness and began squeezing and stroking it. He pushed her against the wall and kissed her again, his hand going down the front of her blouse then, with a groan, he simply tore it open, sending buttons flying all over the floor with a light, musical rattle.

She landed on his bed, still in her panties, her legs parted and her lips plump and bruised from his kisses. His hands delved into her panties, then found the center of her wetness and began running his finger expertly over her nub. He pulled the panties upward, a quick hard yank that took them deep into the cleft between her cheeks and labia. His thumb pressed hard against her clit, making her cry out.

"Damn, you're sexy, Joy," he murmured as he watched her face.

Her teeth ran along her lower lip as she tried to keep her eyes open against his touch. She grabbed his hand and flicked it away, surprising him for a moment.

She took advantage of his momentary hesitation and pushed him onto his back. She stood and stripped her panties off, his green eyes unable to leave her body. She noticed his breath hitch and grinned as she climbed back on the bed, stalking him like a cat, her mouth moved over his skin, tasting it, and licking it.

She took him into her mouth and down her throat, her lips tightening around his hardened flesh. He grabbed handful of her hair, muttered out, "Oh fuck, Joy, do that, please," as his hips arched up higher against her face.

Her tongue swirled along the shaft and her head bobbed. He was thick and large, larger than any man she had ever known and she had to struggle for breath, but once she got it she settled into a rhythm that had him moaning sharply.

His hands tugged at her hair again, and before she could protest she landed on her back and Hawk moved along her body, his mouth trailing fiery kisses along her skin.

His mouth went to her center. Her core spilled fluids across his face and tongue as his fingers thrust deeply within her, and his tongue massaged her clit in a maddening way that had her squirming and flailing, her heels digging deeply into the mattress as she tried to get her ass up in the air in order to give him a better angle of penetration into her body.

Her cries were wild and loud. She wasn't normally a vocal lover, but words came tripping off her tongue, words she would have been embarrassed to say to anyone else as she begged him to let her come, to fuck her, and hard.

He didn't listen. He crooked his fingers and thrust further within her, finding her G-spot and stimulating it. Her whole body came off the bed, arcing high as an orgasm so intense she nearly fainted hit her and sent bolts of sheer, decadent pleasure running through her.

Her body vibrated with pleasure as he moved upwards, her juices glistening on his face and fingers. He thrust inside her quickly. His hardness filled her, opening her and allowing him to slide past her slick walls.

Her hands gripped his shoulders desperately as her legs wound around his waist. His fingers slid under her hips and tilted them higher, then he positioned himself up on his forearms and withdrew just to drive into her again, a hard, fast pump that sent her spinning back toward ecstasy.

He swung his hips from side to side, and his fingers went back to her clit. He ran his fingers around it in a slow, tormenting circle as he withdrew then entered her again.

Sweating, gasping, and stunned by the thrills coursing through her body, all Joy could do was hang on as he made love to her, taking her to yet another orgasm and the long splendid aftershocks that made her quiver and moan.

She felt him come. She felt his hot seed splash into her body and she cried out, her swollen inner folds clenching and loosening around his hot flesh, cradling him and releasing him as he thrust a few more times and then lay still.

They lay there, trying to catch their breath. Their mingled fluids dripped from her body, and that was when she realized that, in their haste, they had forgotten the condom.

Hawk noticed it too. "Shit. Joy, I'm so sorry. I never forget."

"It's okay. I'm on birth control."

Or was she? In order to get the surgery, she'd had to stop taking it, but the doctor had sworn it would stay in her system for a long time since she'd been on it for so many years.

What was done was done and she wasn't willing to let such a splendid moment be ruined, so she pushed that aside as he slowly withdrew from her. His now-flaccid member left a thin trail of fluids across her upper thigh and he pulled her close, so close her head rested on his chest and she could hear the sound of his heartbeat on her ear. It was a comforting sound, and she closed her eyes to hear it.

Then he moved slightly so that his head was on her breast. She held her breath. That awful ticking sound...

She muttered that and he said, "I like it. It means you're here to be with me right now, right here."

His finger went to her scar and traced it. "That's what all of this means. I know some people think scars are hideous and ugly, but I don't. Some of the most beautiful people have scars. They're like tattoos in a way; they tell their own story."

She let that wash over her. Tears stung her eyes. She knew damn well Pixie had set them up, and she was grateful that she had.

Hawk was nothing like any man she had ever met before, ever.

Suddenly wanted to tell him everything. Who she really was. Who her father was and who her mother and siblings were. She wanted to tell him and then forget about it. Just let it be one more thing about her like her scar and that weird ticking noise that came from her heart.

Only it wasn't like those things.

Not at all.

CHAPTER 12

They lay tangled together in the bed. Sweat dried on their bodies, and the smell of sex hung in the air. Joy traced the ripples of his six-pack and absently started talking, "I like your house, by the way."

He smiled. "Me too. It's not far from Van Nuys, geographically, but it's a long way in every other way."

"You grew up in Van Nuys?"

He nodded. "Yes. How about you?"

"No, sorry." Her mouth went to his nipples in an effort to distract him. It worked, to her delight.

He brushed her hair back from her face and pressed against her, the already stiffening flesh of his member pushing against the skin of her upper thighs momentarily.

She brought her lips to his mouth and after a long kiss, she asked, "Did you do the art yourself?" She pointed to the detailed drawing above his bed.

"Most of it, but not all. If I didn't love tattooing so much I might give painting as a profession a try, but I think I'm okay for now." He chuckled, as if embarrassed to admit it.

"Your work's stunning." She slowly trailed a finger up his side and near his armpit, teasing. She said, "You could always do what that other famous tattoo guy did and start to making tee shirts and shoes and stuff."

He laughed and squirmed under her finger. "Um, no thanks. He's a great artist. I love his tats. I hated his clothes, and was glad when they went out of style."

She tilted her head. "Are you going to tattoo until you retire?"

"Or until I don't want to do it anymore. That's my plan. I know things happen. You lose your hands or your eyes, or just the love of doing it. But the shop will go on, anyway, as long as the lease stands."

She looked into his face. "You worry about it?"

He frowned. "Not really. I have a plan for that too. Right now the landlord won't sell, but he will eventually, and when he does I intend to buy it."

"What if he runs it up on you?"

Hawk trailed a hand slowly up and down her back. "Smart question, but I've a backup plan. I'm hoping not to have to use it, but I do have one."

"Always smart to have a backup plan." She began to press her hips against the side of his to the movement of his hand on her back.

"I agree. So what's yours?"

She burst into laughter. "I must not be that smart."

He lifted an eyebrow. "Really? No backup plan?"

She shook her head. "No, none. I never wanted anything else. All I ever wanted was to build houses, or to make them beautiful. I wanted to make them pretty for other people."

"Why?"

She bit her lips and admitted something she didn't expect. "I guess I'm just hoping to put something beautiful into the world. There's enough ugliness."

He cuddled her close. His hardness still nudged at her leg, and she wanted him to make love to her again. She let him kiss her, wanting to get lost in the heat building inside of her, but doubts set in again. She wanted to tell him who she was. She wanted to tell him everything and ask him everything about himself. She knew she couldn't be as open with him as she wanted to be, or learn as much about him as she would like, because if she asked questions about his life, he would ask questions about hers. It was only natural, and fair. They barely knew each other, and to go down that road might change everything now.

The whole thing between them was so new, and so precious. She just wanted to keep it that way for a little while longer. She just wanted it to stay uncomplicated and easy and oh-so-beautiful for just a little while longer.

She would tell him. She would.

Very soon.

Just not right now.

CHAPTER 13

Before Joy realized, eight weeks had flown right by. She couldn't see Hawk a lot; they both had long hours of work that didn't always leave available at the same time, but they talked almost daily and a few times he even Skyped her from the shop. He made her laugh, and when they were together his touch inflamed her senses and his kindness sealed off what was left of the hurt from Brian.

It felt like she was beginning to blossom and spread her wings, for the first time in her life. She started saying no to the dreaded and hated lunch dates with her mother. It shocked and angered her mother, but Joy found she didn't care. She knew the lunches were toxic to her, and always had been. She had gone out of a sense of duty, but her mother never had a compliment for her or something nice to say. As time passed, Hawk kept finding new ways to delight her and explore her body, and she began to see her body not as a cumbersome vehicle but as a sleek and well-designed beauty capable of bringing pleasure. He made her feel attractive, and she gained confidence in herself, something she had precious little of before.

She knew it was not all due to Hawk, but his words and looks gave her confidence. Her work was moving forward since the purchase of the empty lots and the houses, and she was caught up in a huge project for pay too. With every small victory came more self-assurance and, one afternoon as she was walking through a store, she noticed men looking at her with appreciation in their eyes. She was startled, and, as she realized, it brought a sense of happiness – not because they were gawking at her, but simply because they were noticing.

Her newfound confidence gave her the ability to walk tall and straight, instead of hunched over and at a hurried pace. She found herself caring less what people thought of her. When she went out to eat, she didn't try to eat slowly to let others finish before she did so she didn't look like the fat girl who rushed through their food greedily. Food suddenly became more pleasant too. She'd always enjoyed it, of course, but going out meant either ordering some healthy option so people would think she was at least trying to curb her weight, or ordering something delicious and decadent with utter guilt running through her because she was sure everyone around was wondering why she didn't order something healthy and more diet-like. She didn't care about her weight. She was tall, not overweight, she exercised and, with how busy she'd been, she had actually lost a few pounds without even trying.

She shed the guilt feeling of food and realized it went back to her childhood, with a mother and step- sisters who made her feel inadequate. She almost told Hawk about it, but caught herself. She didn't press him about his family and he didn't say much about it either.

He'd asked her and she'd brushed it off with a casual, "Oh they're like every other family, I guess." While it wasn't an outright lie, it was still a lie.

She worried and fretted about it constantly in the back of her mind. She felt guilty that she hadn't told Hawk who her family was, but now that she'd kept it a secret it felt like it would be worse admitting it.

It wasn't like he wouldn't find out eventually. The longer she held it off, the more she began to worry about his reaction when he did. It wasn't just that she had lied about it either.

Hawk didn't regret doing that reality show, but he was not at all willing to get caught back up in anything like it ever again. When he had told her that one night, she'd nearly admitted who she was and then held back. Hawk and Lily's ex, Mark had a sort of casual friendship. Hawk wasn't much for going out to parties and he wasn't into the whole rock-n-roll Hollywood scene either.

They had been having a drink at a sports bar not far from the tattoo shop when Lily's reality show started on one of the TVs.

"I know the guy in this show." Hawk pointed up to the screen.

Joy nearly choked on her beer. "Y-You do?"

"He was on my show a couple times and we've gone out for beers after. It's a shame."

"What is?" Joy tried to ignore the pounding sound rushing between her ears.

"Mark was willing to work through all his issues."

Joy swallowed, feeling like a fly caught in a spider web. "I don't really watch the show. What issues?"

"Drinking, drugs, womanizing. All that shit. He might've stood a change at getting clean and being faithful to his wife. But that show... that's what ruined him in the first place. His ex doesn't see it. That damn show intruded on their lives on a constant basis. It was the poor guy's undoing."

Joy shrugged. "Show or no show, he should have stopped or gone for help."

"He wanted to." Hawk leaned forward and shook his head. "Mark's kind of like me in a way. He didn't want the spotlight. He married into that family. Seeing his wife screaming at him, hearing her screaming at him is one thing. But having everyone in the world be privy to their problems and labeling him the bad guy no matter how hard he was trying is another. He was forever rushing to console Lily and then being reminded all the time how lousy a husband he was, how his failures day after day ruined her. It finally got to be too much for Mark to take. I feel bad for the guy."

Joy could understand that. She really could. She'd often thought the same thing herself. Except, she'd never met Mark; at least not when he was sober enough to remember her. She worried guiltily that she might run into him at Hawk's shop.

"He's gotten himself straightened out on his own, thank goodness."

"Really?" Joy hadn't heard about it. Then again, Lily wouldn't tell her, and she hadn't been on a luncheon in months so she wouldn't have any idea anyways.

"Yeah, his band's headed out on a world tour."

"Good for him." She heaved a huge sigh of relief. But the main issue remained unspoken. Hawk was not at all interested in being a part of Hollywood, and her family was Hollywood in all its tattered glory. She stayed out of it, but it didn't mean that it wouldn't eventually come looking for her.

And she was terrified that he would find out and leave her when it did.

CHAPTER 14

Hawk had never been happier. He was nearing thirty, and for the first time in his life everything felt right. It was because of Joy. He'd never met anyone like her. She was gorgeous, intelligent, and she was fast with a quip or joke. She was slowly becoming more confident and bold every day, and he loved that about her. It was like watching a rose bloom from a tight bud into a thing of full-blown beauty.

Tinkerbelle laughter caught his attention and brought him back to the present. Pixie sat in his shop that day, and he had a feeling she was here because of Cliff. He wanted to ask but he knew she would just deny it. However, Hawk knew she couldn't deny the way her eyes travelled straight to his work room when she came in, or the way she watched him while he helped other customers.

Pixie really was like his little sister, and he wanted to see her happy. Cliff wasn't a terrible guy, but he certainly liked the ladies, and they liked him right back.

Hawk didn't want to see Pixie get hurt, and he was considering telling her that while he worked yet another butterfly into the skin near the bottom of her slender right leg.

Her laughter had caught his attention, and she grinned when he looked up at her. "Are you and Joy going out tonight again?"

'We are. Aren't you living with her again?"

Pixie chuckled. "I never really move out. I just go somewhere else for a little while. My new job sucks so hard I can't really afford my own place right now anyway."

"You mean you can't afford it because you keep blowing your money on saving some little animal."

"Hey, I helped keep a Pitbull alive this week. I have a place to stay, but it was totally homeless."

"I know. I saw the video." He chuckled, tempted to rub the top of her head and tussle her newly-colored purple hair. "You do good work, Pixie, and the world's a better place for it, but you do know that eventually you're going to have to become adult at some point too, don't you?"

"I do adult," she huffed. "I really do. I just can't stand to see so much unhappiness in the world. It's terrible and it hurts my heart."

He smiled fondly. "I know. It's okay."

"Besides, Joy understands. She won't take my rent money, though, so I'm always finding things to get her. Just the other day I donated my rent in her name to this great rescue."

He hid a smile. "I'm sure she appreciated that. And I am also sure she doesn't really need your money or for you to donate it to a rescue. Maybe you'd be better off putting it into the bank so you could buy a house or something adult like that."

"She definitely doesn't need it. Her trust fund's worth ten million."

Hawk stared at Pixie, sure he'd heard her wrong. "What did you just say?"

Pixie's head was bent over, her purple hair swinging around her face. She looked up and said, "I'm just saying that you would never even know she was so rich, or that she's the daughter of some big-shot movie producer. It's like it's no big deal. She's just like everyone else, and she doesn't have a snobby bone in her body."

He blinked a few times, his breath suddenly lost somehow. "What the hell are you talking about?" He set the tattoo gun down and rested his fists on his knees as he pushed his chair away to stare at Pixie.

She suddenly looked stricken. "Oh shit! She didn't tell you, did she?" Her eyes filled. "Please don't tell her I said anything.

Fuck! I've never told anyone before. I only told you because I assumed she had. She likes you, I mean *really* likes you. She trusts you, so I just assumed..."

"She didn't." The words were hard and inflexible. He felt bad for Pixie, but anger boiled below it toward someone else. "I was under the impression she's estranged from her family."

"At least she told you that." Pixie sighed and rubbed her forehead. "She is, but it's polite. It's all fucked if you ask me. She sees them from time to time but... they're all idiots. They treat her like shit. Well, her dad's okay but her sisters and brother, and her mom's the worst! Those people are heinous. No wonder she wants nothing to do with them."

Hawk said nothing. He couldn't process the thought that Joy hadn't told him this. After everything he'd told her.

Pixie went on, "She asked me to go with her one day to see her family. They have some lunch thing they do once a month. It was friggin' awful. I couldn't believe how they walked all over her feelings and acted like the things she's accomplished, and in such a short time too, are so stupid or mean nothing. She's not into Hollywood, and, to them, she's a big disappointment and embarrassment. No wonder she's so messed up."

Hawk had to concede to Pixie's last point. Joy's self-esteem was shaky at best, but he'd watched it grow lately and was proud of her, and *for* her, too. But all this...?

Damn it! He was pissed because she'd lied to him.

Had she really lied to him?

Not exactly. She'd said she didn't get along with her family and tried not to see them. Pixie had just said the same thing. What ticked him off was that she hadn't trusted him enough to tell him who her family was. "Who's her family?"

Pixie stared at him and knew better than to lie. "Tyler Reed's her dad."

His mouth fell open. Tyler Reed was ruthless and sadistic for the most part. They said he had a soft spot for his family, but if he did Hawk couldn't imagine it. His wife, Megan, was a cold and demanding woman who'd shown up more than once on her daughter's reality show. No, stepdaughter.

Lily.

His lip curled. He actually knew Lily very well. She'd hit on him more than once and when he had pointed out that her husband was not just a client, but a friend, she'd sneered out, "Well, he fucks who he wants, so why can't I?"

The whole family was a big hot mess of drug addiction and greed. How in the hell had Joy, his Joy, wound up with them? Had they adopted her or something?

Why the hell hadn't she told him?

His lips pressed tightly together. She should have told him. He'd asked her not to lie, and she hadn't, not exactly, but when he'd asked her pointed questions she had evaded them; while that wasn't lying, it was close enough for him. "She should have told me."

Pixie shook her head. "Her last boyfriend pretended he didn't want anything from her, and then when he realized she didn't want to help him meet and charm her dad into giving him a part, he dumped her. You can't tell her I told you that either if she hasn't told you. It was painful, and right after she had the surgery." She dropped her head and forced Hawk to look her in the eye. "You can see why she's gun-shy."

"It doesn't excuse the point—"

"When she went into the hospital, I was the only one there," Pixie cut him off. "Her parents were in the South of France and they sent flowers, but they didn't come back. They said the surgeon had assured them it wasn't life-threatening." Her eyes met his. Tears gathered on her lashes. "Joy said it wasn't either, but...but they cracked her chest open and took her heart out, Hawk, and the only person in the waiting room was *me*. That's how much her family cares about her."

He stared at her, unsure of what to say.

"I'm sorry she didn't tell you, but you can see why, right? They might not hate her, but they sure don't seem to love her either. All they've ever done is cause her pain." Pixie shook her head, her hair swinging in each direction as she moved. "Every time she dates a guy, she always has to wonder if he's dating her, or her family."

Hawk could understand. Except he wasn't that kind of guy. It ticked him off that Joy thought he might be. "I can see that. But we're...I mean, I'm in it for her, not to get famous or rich or...shit." He threw his hands up and ran his fingers through his hair. "I just don't see why she can't trust me!"

"She does," Pixie said.

"No, not all the way."

Pixie swallowed hard. "Look let's do this. Let's pretend I never said anything and that you aren't mad at her for something so silly."

He glared at her. "It isn't silly."

"No, but none of who her family is or how they treat her or why she doesn't tell people is either," Pixie said. "It's really hurt her over the years. She's leery. Wouldn't you be?"

He could understand that. But he'd thought they'd gotten to a place where they could trust each other. He'd shared his secrets with her, and now he felt angry that she hadn't seen fit to share with him.

He'd believed they'd gotten closer than that. Maybe he was more into her than she was into him.

Pixie chewed her lower lip. "Please tell me you won't say anything to her."

That wasn't a promise he wanted to make, but this wasn't Pixie's fault. He'd give Joy a chance to tell him.

What if she didn't?

"Fine. I won't say anything." *For now.*

Pixie threw her arms around him and gave him a tight hug. "Thanks, Hawk."

She scurried out and he began to clean up the room, dropping the gun into cleaning solution and wiping down the bed with disinfectant before loading out the trash. Uneasiness settled into him. Maybe Joy needed a chance to be honest with him, and he would keep his promise not to tell her that Pixie had blabbed her secret, but he was determined to find out if she trusted him or not.

That's all that mattered to him. Trust.

If Joy didn't trust him, he was wasting his time. If he couldn't trust her...

He'd grown up in a house with a father who lied constantly and a mother who knew it and just went along with the lies, never really understanding how badly it hurt the entire family.

His father lied about his affairs. Lied about the money he'd spent on gambling. The debts they owed and what bills he had payed. He lied about everything, all the time. Hawk loved his father in a way, but he had zero respect for him.

He couldn't be around him for much time without getting angry, and the old wounds never healed. He often wished they could, but he knew part of the reason that they hadn't was because his father still lied.

Still lied about the unpaid bills, drinking, gambling, and sleeping around. Lies that his current wife, like Hawk's mother, chose to believe. It was a shitty thing to do, lying to people who cared about you, and Hawk swore he would never do it.

He'd also sworn he would never put up with lying either.

He knew Joy hadn't lied outright, but in his book a lie was a lie, even if it was a lie just because she didn't say the whole truth. White lies were lies. There was no grey, just black or white.

Hawk drilled the trash into the bin out back and headed back inside. There was one thing he could do to fix this. He'd press her and see what she said.

He swallowed the lump of disgust building in his stomach. It made him feel sneaky and dishonest. However, Joy hiding it from him meant that she had secrets. He couldn't date someone who hid from the truth.

His thoughts were interrupted by Joy's arrival. She came through the door in a floaty little dress that had a hem that doubled in on itself and swirled around her knees.

His body burned with desire. She didn't like to wear dresses because she didn't think they looked pretty on her, and the fact that she had one on, and that she'd undoubtedly put it on because he'd told her he would love to see her in one, hit him hard.

And so did guilt.

He'd plotted to catch her in a lie to force her to tell him the truth, and in she walks with her hair down, flowing around her waist, pink gloss on her lush lovely mouth, and that damn stunning dress covering her gorgeous body. All to please him.

Okay, I'm an asshole. But thankfully I've been an asshole in my head and not to her.

That made him feel slightly better. At least he hadn't made a total idiot of himself.

That didn't assuage his feelings about what Pixie had told him, however, and when she walked up to him her smile faltered. "Are you okay?"

He nodded. "Yeah, it's just been a weird day."

"Oh no, what happened?"

"Oh the usual. I finished Pixie's butterflies."

"She told me you were. She hasn't been home yet. I can't wait to see them."

He wanted to crush her to his chest and ask her why she hadn't told him, and at the same time he wanted to say nothing. It was such an odd thing and situation he didn't know how to handle it. Finally, he said, "You look gorgeous! How about we get out of here?"

"Absolutely! Do you want to go to Santa Monica? I really like Baldi's, and wasn't sure if you'd ever tried there."

He nodded. "I have. I really love their ravioli."

"Me too." His hand caught hers as they walked out of the shop. "I brought the bike, so how about you follow me to my house and I'll grab my car and drive?"

She smiled. "That sounds great. I'd hate driving all the way over there by myself. No one to keep me company." She winked slyly.

He chuckled. "I don't know why. You drive like freaking Batman. I'm grabbing the seat more than your knee."

Her laughter was robust and tinkling. "Why, thank you, I think. No, thank you. In L.A. that means something good."

"It does." He smiled too. His anger had faded and so did the embarrassment at his thoughts. It would be so easy to pretend the conversation with Pixie had never happened at all.

He headed for his bike and she went to her car. His house lay between the restaurant and the shop, and when they pulled into the driveway he put his bike in the garage, and she pulled her car up behind the gate after he pulled the Mustang out.

He opened her door for her and she smiled as she got in. They turned toward Santa Monica and Hawk turned the radio on. It would be easier to sit and listen to the music than try to talk. He didn't trust himself not to ask her about her family. An eighties station played rock songs they both knew, and thankfully distracted him during the car ride.

CHAPTER 15

Lily!

No, no no! Please no! Go away! Go, go go!

Joy froze in horror.

Lily, obviously drunk, was heading straight for them! Unable to think of anything else, Joy seriously considered diving below the table and hiding, but she knew it was too late for that.

Lily plunked her wineglass down on the table and leaned over it. Her dress, a stunning black lace creation, clung to every lean curve like it had been sewn together right there on her body. Her raven hair tumbled free behind a jeweled headband, and her legs, made longer by lethally-high stilettos, shone with the healthy tan she kept by perfectly calibrating her time in a spray tan salon. "Wellll..." Lily said, "No wonder you didn't want me to ask him to come on my show. You tart!" She laughed loudly and drew stares to their table.

Hawk's face was tight with anger. "Hello, Lily."

She laughed and elegantly sat down into a chair, amazing for how drunk she seemed. She dragged it closer to Hawk and the table and leaned forward. Her face was made up perfectly, her lips slicked with a deep matte crimson and her eyes accented by a single flick of eyeliner. Her voice dropped to a sexy tone, "Hello, Handsome-Hawk. I haven't seen you in a long time. Are you still helping my ex get laid by your shared groupies?"

Joy's face burned, probably a deep red crimson. "Lily," she hissed.

Hawk crossed his arms over his chest. "I don't do groupies." His words held anger, and his demeanor had turned icy. "You're really drunk, Lily. I don't think now's a good time."

"What? I can't talk to my *darling* snobby sister?"

Joy's face heated hotter, she was sure it was going to blow right off her head. She expected shock or surprise from Hawk.

But there was none.

Her eyes were glued to him as he spoke, "Lily, you can talk to her another time. We're obviously trying to have dinner here, and you're in the way."

Lily leaned back. Her eyes narrowed yet again as she spun around to face Joy. She grabbed her wine, oblivious of the spill on the white tablecloth. "You know, I should've known you were trying to hit on him yourself that day at lunch."

"I—" Joy started, but Lily cut her off.

"When else do you care what I do on my show?"

Hawk snorted. "Nobody cares what you do on your show, Lily. That's the reason they're about to cancel it."

Lily glowered at him. "They aren't going to cancel it."

Hawk stared at her, his gaze never wavering. "I'm sure they will."

Lily stood and started to walk away, then paused long enough to deliver a death blow. She patted Joy's shoulder. "At least you get my leftovers. He hit on me and luckily I said no. I would hate for you to have my sloppy seconds." She walked away, a deliberate sway to her hips.

Joy took a deep, pained breath. Her eyes went back to Hawk's face. She had some explaining to do, but, instead, she said, "You hit on her?"

"Not even remotely."

His face glowered with anger. He'd already known Lily was her sister. When? For how long?

She stared down at the table, "I...I don't know what to say."

"Don't say anything."

Her lips compressed. "You weren't surprised she's my sister?"

He said, way too calmly for her liking, "I already knew."

Her heart shattered in her chest. Tears stung her eyes. "You did?"

"I found out earlier today."

Earlier today? Her lips twisted. "Pixie."

He didn't say anything. He didn't have to.

She sighed and tossed her napkin onto the table. "I should've told you. I wanted to. For weeks I wondered how to, I just didn't know how. You...you're the first person I really believed liked me for me and I didn't want that to change."

"Do you honestly think that would change just because you happen to be related to them?"

The tears escaped down her cheeks. "Things have changed because of that before."

"No, they didn't. If someone changed things because of who your family is, then they weren't there anyway, at least not in the way they should've been."

She looked down. It was all crumbling down around her, and she couldn't find any balance no matter how hard she tried. "How...where do we go from here?" She figured he'd drive her home and it would be the end of it. He had no use for Hollywood or its people.

Hawk scoffed. "We order dessert."

She looked at him. She wanted to believe that it would all be okay; that it didn't really matter who she was, or who her family was, or that she hadn't told him, but she knew it did matter. "I'm sorry. I did want to tell you."

"Would you have told me?"

She picked up her napkin and tangled it with her fingers. She nodded, hard. "Yes. I mean...I only didn't tell you because...because I was afraid." She sucked in a sharp breath. "I know that's not your fault and you haven't done anything to deserve it... I have a lot to work on, and I know it. I'm trying. It's just that..."

His hand came across the table and took hers. "Joy, I can't imagine what life with that crew must have been like. Mark used to talk about your family, and he always said he couldn't stand any of them except her youngest sister, who hardly ever came around because she couldn't stand them either."

Mark? He hardly knew her.

"Maybe I should've put it together myself. I mean, you definitely should've told me. When Pixie mentioned it, I was pissed, I'm not going to lie, but I was pissed because I felt like you had lied to me. Maybe not outright, but...anyway, it hit me pretty fast how stupid and childish I was being. I'm not normally stupid or childish, and I didn't like it."

"I'm so sorry." He was going to dump her. She just knew it.

"Now here we are. It's out in the open. Your sister's a witch and she really messed up part of our date, but we don't have to let all of this screw up the rest of it."

Wait. What?

His fingers were warm and strong as he squeezed her hand. His words hit her right in her heart. She said, "You're right, we don't."

"I know what you need."

She blinked. "You do?"

His grin got wider. "I do. Let's get out of here."

"Are you suggesting we..." Her gazed dropped as she licked her lips.

He chuckled. "Oh, hell yes, but later. I want to show you something."

He gestured to the waiter, who came over with the check. He paid and they left in his Mustang, heading into the heart of L.A.

Joy stared out the windows for a while then asked, "Where are we going?"

"To see my old house."

She lifted an eyebrow. "Your old house?"

"Yeah."

She watched him, trying to read his face, but couldn't figure out anything. He seemed angry or upset, but she wasn't sure. "Are you mad at me?"

He shook his head. "Not anymore."

"I'm still kind of mad at me. I did mean to tell you. I just got scared."

"Did it ever occur to you that all people get used at some point, Joy?"

She blinked. "What?" She wasn't sure what he was getting at.

"You aren't the only one who's been used by someone. When I first started tattooing, I had no idea that the guys who hung out around the shops all day weren't there because they thought we were cool guys. The other guys knew. I thought...well, I thought I was like that guy who tatted in my neighbor's garage. That people thought I was cool and sort of ...I don't know."

She slipped her hand into his, realizing he had things in his past he didn't like talking about either.

"Before I knew it I had a full day almost every day, but no paying clients. I was just being the cool tat guy who'd let you ride his chair for no fee. The guy who'd taken me in and trained me eventually came to me and asked if I liked eating. Of course I said yes. So he said that I'd better cut the dead brush off my money tree."

Her face colored. She'd never considered that he might know exactly what it was like to be used for what he had to offer. She'd never been used by her family, just embarrassed by them and used by others to get to her family. It was the same thing, really. "I see. I didn't consider that. You seem so put together. Like you've never been any other way. I guess I was just so narrow-sighted because...well, because I grew up in a way that was all about people using each other."

"What do you mean?" he asked quietly.

"People would come to our house when Dad wasn't home to talk to Mom about getting them into whatever project he was on.

She would strike this kind of deal that would get her what she wanted, and then she would get Dad to do whatever, and in return he would get to blow off her boring parties. It was all bribery and using each other. Nothing was for free."

Hawk sighed. "Everything comes at a price."

"I'd watch it happen at Dad's office too. I mean, the way they talked about these people. They're famous, and all that, but they're still people. They talked about them like they weren't. Like their lives and feelings had no meaning. Just pieces on a chess board and everyone else would be moving them all around. I've seen my dad wreck someone's career just because he didn't like them personally, or use someone to get what he wanted and then dump them. I've seen a lot of people do it, and after it happened to me a few times I just didn't want it to happen anymore. Or at least be around it. So I basically ran away. Disappeared."

Hawk squeezed her hand. "Nobody wants it to happen to them, Joy, that's the thing. But it does. We can't know what people really think of or want from us. It's always a risk. You have to be willing to trust. The thing that bothers me the most, bothered me, really, because I really am over it, is that at any time you could have told me."

"I know. I should have. Time just kinda got away from me."

"I'll make you a deal. I won't keep secrets from you if you promise not to keep any from me."

She took a long breath. "Deal." She tilted her head. "Wait. Are you keeping secrets?"

"I'm not keeping any that I wouldn't be willing to share with you. There's a lot of things we haven't told each other, but that's because we haven't had a chance." He leaned down and kissed her sweetly on the lips. "Now we can really talk and maybe get to know each other in an even deeper way than before."

"I'd like that," she said. Her throat hurt from holding back tears. He was such a good man, and she had almost wrecked everything over something so silly and trivial. To her it had been such a huge thing, and now that she saw how silly it was she was stricken with remorse. She was also determined not to keep anything else from him. Ever.

"Ah, here we are." Hawk stopped the car. He hesitated a moment and then got out of the car. She followed him and stared in surprise. The house was a wreck. It had burned at some point, evidence of a bad fire everywhere. The neighborhood was tough and dangerous. She could almost smell the danger simmering along the streets.

Hawk sighed. "So here's where I grew up. My dad's a drunk. And a gambler. And a womanizer. He's the biggest liar who ever walked the earth too. My mom's great. She worked two and sometimes even three jobs to keep us fed and in clothes and shelter. She busted her ass because our dad wouldn't or couldn't deal with life on its terms."

Joy ignored the tear that slid down her cheek. She'd thought she had it rough. She'd been blind.

"She should have left him but she didn't. He started that fire a year ago. He was drunk and smoking a cigarette when he went to bed. Burned the whole damn house down. He nearly died. My mom nearly died too.

"And that was what it took to get her to wise up and finally leave his ass, as sad as that is."

"I'm so sorry, Hawk."

"No, don't be. My dad's a great guy. He just can't keep his shit together. I love him but I don't respect him, and I don't have to. He hasn't earned that respect and it can't be just given; it has to be earned. Maybe that's why we butt heads so much. He thinks I'm supposed to respect him just because he's my dad, and I think I should respect him as a man and I can't because I don't see how he ever was a man." He leaned against the hood of the car and stared at the decrepit house. "A real man doesn't cheat or lie or let his family go without. A real man isn't tough the way my dad is. To my dad, it's all about having a big dick and using it. Or having fists and not being afraid to use them. I think a real man should be a man who knows when to walk away from something, and when to have sex, and who to have it with." His gaze swung over to her. "I think real men fall in love and cry and get a little crazy sometimes. They have feelings that they aren't afraid to show. My dad thinks real men are stoic and take everything and internalize it then turn it into whatever they have to in order to get through it all."

Joy's chest expanded and constricted. "I like your ideas better."

Hawk nodded. "Me too. My dad let his disappointments and ideas ruin his life. He almost ruined ours too. He wanted to be an actor. He was an actor, in fact. He played in half a dozen really bad movies right around the time my mom started having us kids, and he never got over that. He somehow always equated us with his failure to launch as a real actor. Every time he had to take a job out here in the real world or didn't get a part, it was somehow all tied up into him settling down and settling for a family instead of going after his dreams."

No wonder he hated Hollywood. Joy leaned against the car beside him, the warmth of the setting sun heating her tush on the black metal of the car. "I'm so sorry for that. I can't imagine why people feel that way. My mom always equated me with the end of her modeling career. And when I wasn't this perfect little girl with a tiny, frail little body and loads of charm, it all got worse. One big disappointment."

Hawk leaned into her and she rested her head on his shoulder. "You're perfect, Joy. Maybe you aren't her idea of perfect, but that doesn't mean you were ever imperfect. The thing is that we don't have to be our parents. Or our old neighborhoods. Or anything else just because that's what someone else thought we should be."

He was right. She nodded. "Yeah."

He tilted his head and said, "Let's get the hell out of here."

They drove away from the burned-out shell of his old home with Joy thinking hard. She wanted to ask him a million questions and she was able to suddenly. "So, where are your mom and dad now?"

"Mom lives over in Greater Valley Glen. She managed to squirrel away a little money here and there and I helped too; so did my siblings. She got a better house between that and the insurance. Dad lives with some waitress he was fucking around with when the fire happened. We haven't met her yet. I don't think he wants us to."

"That sucks." She didn't know what else to say.

He chuckled. "It kinda does. I don't think he'll stay with her very long either. He's in AA and he's been trying for acting parts lately. He's still a good-looking guy. He's a little clearer these days and I think he knows he won't ever get that big break, but only because he has finally come to grips with the fact that whatever chance he had, he blew it in the bars and during his binges in Vegas. Not that he'll ever admit that out loud." He reached over and rested his hand on her knee. "I'm glad he's trying, though. Everyone should have a dream. I just don't think they should let that dream get in the way of everyone in their lives. Speaking of dreams, how goes the project?"

She made a face. "I'm still a little stuck, although I hate to admit it. The problem is the houses need to be renovated. That's not a huge problem, except if I do too much renovation they will cause the neighborhood to go up in value, which I want eventually, just not that fast. If I do the houses too fancy, I run the risk of them being too big of a blow to my budget, and I'll have to take a major loss to my own pocket. I don't really mind that, because I can afford some loss, but what I can't afford is for everyone in the neighborhood to expect that same level in every house. When they don't get it, they won't buy in. That'll take the whole thing down. So I'm trying to find a way to keep costs down while still making things nice."

Hawk pulled the car over and put it into park, turned, and put his arm on the back rest of her seat. "I know you have great contacts with wholesalers and stuff, but there is another route, and one you probably haven't considered."

She asked, "What?"

"Well I had to have some stuff in my house and Mom's replaced, but I had a really tight budget so I went to this shop... it's like a salvage place. When the more upscale houses get redone they don't always destroy the stuff they take out. Like cabinets and counters and so on. They all go to this second-hand kind of shop. Habitat for Care, I think it's called. Have you considered buying stuff from there?"

Her mouth fell open. "No. I didn't even know the place existed."

He chuckled. "I have a customer who's a contractor and he told me about it. It's like a dirty little secret. Every contractor takes stuff they can get a few bucks for down there, and since the homeowners just want it gone and pay to get it gone, they never really ask questions about it. You could probably get some really decent stuff for a damn good price there."

"Holy hot cakes! How did I not know this? Could you take me down there? Now?"

He laughed. "I'm pretty sure they're closed right now but, yeah, absolutely." His hand tickled the back of her neck. "Holy hot cakes?"

She grinned at him and shrugged. "I was just describing you."

His eyebrows rose. "Really?"

She sat back, relief filling her as she absently waved her hand at him. If Hawk was right about the shop, that could solve so many of her current problems. "How about we go first thing in the morning?"

"Sure."

She leaned over and kissed him sweetly on the lips. "Thank you for being so wonderful."

He laughed. "Oh, I'm sure someone would've told you about it sooner or later."

"But not everyone would believe in what I'm trying to do."

Hawk started the car and pulled back out onto the road. "In case you didn't notice, I grew up in a neighborhood just like the one you're trying to work in. I do get it. I would've loved for someone to come in and try to do what you're trying to do. I'm sure most of the families on our block would've felt the same way. They still will. It's hard in L.A. when you live in the neighborhoods nobody wants to live in because they aren't filled with the rich and famous and the best schools or whatever. Everyone outside L.A. thinks everyone here is rich and happy, and you have this pressure to keep it going—that stupid myth. It would help a lot if that was in the slightest bit true."

He was perfect. So perfect. She was so crazy in love with him. It hit her hard, right then and there. She was in love with Hawk Reynolds. She hadn't wanted to admit it to herself and she was afraid to say it to him, for fear saying it would somehow shatter that spell.

"Would you like me to stay the night? I mean, that way I can take you to the contractor place tomorrow morning before I head over to the shop."

She nodded, not bothering to mention that her car was at his place. She grinned, giddy with her realization that she was in love with him. *Damn, I'm going to tell him too!* "I would like that a lot. Do you know, Hawk Reynolds, that you are beyond perfect? It scared the hell out of me when you asked me out because, well, you're the kind of guy all women want but never touch. I mean, you're stupid hot. You're not cocky, but super sweet, and kind. And you've got that great sense of humor and your own business, and I just couldn't figure out why you would want to date me of all people. And you're hot. Panty-melting hot."

He laughed. "Joy, I was thinking the very same things, only in reverse or vice versa or whatever. I don't have a college education. I don't have much to offer but a tattoo business and a set of abs. At least that was how I saw it. But I think we do a good job of being together."

She said, "Yes, we do. A damn good job."

"You're boxer-meltin' hot too—whatever the hell that is. You're hot, dammit." He grinned wickedly as his hand slid up her thigh and under her dress.

"Can this hunk of metal go any faster?" she urged as she rotated her hips closer to his hand.

CHAPTER 16

"I promise my room's not a mess this time," Joy said as she giggled and tried to get the front door unlocked. Hawk had one hand inside the top of her dress while his lips were doing provocative things to her ear and neck.

"Is Pixie home?" he mumbled.

"Her car's gone."

"Good."

The door lock finally clicked and Joy pushed the door open. She tugged Hawk's hand out of her bra and slipped her hand into his, pulling him toward her room.

He glanced around quickly when he flicked the light on to her room. "Nice. Though I kinda miss the mess from that first night. How about we mimic it?" He ripped his shirt off and tossed it on the floor. His pants followed suit.

Joy laughed and pulled her dress off, tossing it in the air so it landed right on Hawk's face. She wore a simple white thong and matching bra.

Hawk balled her dress up and threw it on the bed. In two steps he was mere inches from her, their bodies brushing each other in sweet torture. He pulled her hair gently, which caused her head to tilt back, leaving her neck exposed. He pressed his lips into the soft, sensitive skin.

Her hands ran along his rippled chest and down into his boxer-briefs. She palmed his hardening flesh and squeezed. "I want you inside me. Now."

He bit her neck at her words, his hands unclasping her bra expertly from behind, and he stepped away to pull it off and then remove his boxers.

Joy couldn't get her thong off fast enough. She stumbled and fell back onto the bed.

Hawk grinned and fell on top of her, his arms breaking his weight as they landed beside her shoulders. He cupped a breast with one hand. "Damn, you're beautiful." Then he captured her mouth.

Her legs found their around his hips and pulled him tight against her. He didn't need any further invitation as he entered her, her body already wet and begging for him.

She moaned and rotated her hips as he slid in and out of her.

"Fuck," he groaned as his pace quickened with her. "Slow down, babe. I don't want to be done before..." He sucked in a sharp breath as he slowed his rapid movement.

"You tell that heat-seeking missile to wait." Joy ran her hand over his hard, clenched abs. Her eyebrows rose as he pulled out. Just as she brought her head toward his, he slipped his hand between her legs.

"This spot belongs to me alone," he whispered fiercely, and began to rub her nub with his thumb while he slipped his finger inside of her.

His words and touch drove her wild. She came quickly, and he grunted. Her body quivered as he pulled his hand away, and before she finished shaking he slid back inside her. His rhythm was hard and fast now. His sharp movements surprised her and she felt her body tightening against his hardness, squeezing the breath out of both of them.

When she came again, he lost control and erupted inside of her, clinging helplessly to her shoulder as waves of aching lust sent him spiraling into sweet oblivion.

He fell beside her and pulled the small blanket at the end of the bed over them. She pushed him onto his side and curved her body around his back and derrière. She slapped his ass playfully. "Now get some sleep, sexy. We have a busy day tomorrow." *I love you,* she added in her head.

CHAPTER 17

Joy stared at the walls of the space with something akin to wonder. It was all there. Countertops, some of them slightly cracked and in need of minor repair, but that was simple enough. The cabinets were of good quality even if they were older and slightly outdated. Doors. Tile. Hardwood flooring and even a few rolls of high-quality carpet that just needed some good deep cleaning to make it look brand new again.

She turned to Hawk with a huge smile filling her face. "You're a miracle-worker."

"No, that was you this morning," he whispered in her ear and then straightened as someone walked by. "I'm just thrifty." He was in love with her; now he just needed to find the perfect time to tell her.

She laughed and said, "I love it. I love this place! Holy crap! Look at the light fixtures!" She went racing down the aisle.

Hawk watched her go, taking in her firm and rounded ass as she went. His grin was mischievous as he caught himself wondering if they would get arrested if he made love to her right there in the aisle. He strolled along behind her and watched as she ran her fingers over lighting fixtures sitting neatly on shelves. He said, "Look, I like that one."

She looked at the 1950s crystal and beaded creation. She blinked a few times. Her mouth opened and closed. He could see her trying to form words. He burst into laughter and her giggles followed. "Yeah that would look great over your dining room table," she chortled.

Hawk threw his hands up in mock horror. "Never."

She licked her lips. "I have a favor to ask you, and you can say no if you want to and I won't mind."

"Okay, ask and we'll see."

"I want to put a wall up around the park. Not a fence, a wall. I want it to be beautiful, though. I was wondering if you'd mind painting it."

He lifted an eyebrow. "I don't know that I'm that good." He wanted to say yes but she'd just hit a slightly sore spot. He loved to paint as much as he loved to tattoo. He just had far less confidence in his painting than he did his tattoo work. He knew he was good but he hadn't had any formal training, and, while he didn't mind displaying his stuff in the shop, she was asking him to put it on display in a much bigger way that he wasn't sure he could handle. "Joy, you do know I'm not a real artist."

"The hell you aren't," she retorted. "You're as real as it gets. You're also amazing, and you're from a neighborhood like that one so you'd know exactly what should be up there."

Her words made something in him, something he'd been holding back for a long time, stir to life. He wanted to do it. He wanted to expand his realm and go for it.

She knew it, and she was giving him a chance to do it.

He grinned and rubbed his hand over his hair. "You got it."

"Damn, you're sexy." She ran her tongue over her lower lip.

Then he pulled her into his arms and kissed her.

When Hawk dropped Joy off at home a few hours later, she walked in to find Pixie sitting on the sofa with a worried expression on her face.

Pixie looked at her, bit her lips, then burst out with, "I accidentally told Hawk who you are. I'm so sorry. I wasn't going to tell you but...but you're my best friend and it was really wrong and I'm so fucking sorry. He won't tell you I told him. I made him promise. But I feel—"

"I know." Joy dropped down beside her friend and patted her knee. "We ran into Lily last night at dinner and you can imagine what happened. Maybe it was fate. Maybe it was the best thing. Don't even worry about it."

Pixie wore a hangdog expression as she asked, "Are you mad at me?"

"No. I know you didn't do it to be mean or to try to cause trouble. I should have told him myself." Joy pulled the pencil she'd stuck behind her ear out and set it on the table. "Besides, I'm really glad he knows."

Pixie clapped her hands. "So I'm off the hook?"

Joy laughed. "Yes, you're off the hook."

Caligula cawed out, "Pixie's insane."

"We know that, "Joy said easily.

Pixie gave the bird the bird. "So, you two okay?"

Joy frowned, pretending to be worried. "I think so. I mean he was really mad at me and I was...I was being my usual neurotic self, but it smoothed out." She started laughing. "We're totally good."

Pixie grinned. "That's because he's a really good guy. I told you he was."

"You were right." Joy looked back down at the drawings in her hand and frowned. "I just wish I had been the one to tell him, and that I'd done it sooner. It was silly."

"Nah. It all worked out." Pixie put her tattooed legs on the coffee table. "Are you going to your dad's birthday party tonight?"

Joy nodded slowly. She'd saw it on her phone calendar this morning and had pretended not to see it. "Before you ask, I didn't ask Hawk if he wanted to go. Not because I'm worried he'll go all Hollywood on me, but because being around my family isn't something I would wish on anyone.'

"Maybe you should take him just for positive reinforcement. He's good for you, Joy. He put some spine in your back."

"Put some spine in my back?" Joy repeated the words with real amusement. "What does that even mean?"

"It means he's good for you, Joy. He's the first person who let you see yourself the way he sees you, or the way I see you. You're a beautiful and successful woman, and an ambitious one in your own way. You've started standing up for yourself, and you're doing it without even having to think about it. He's somehow made you feel like what you are, which is brave and important, and that matters a whole lot."

Joy smiled, thinking of how much fun they had in bed together. "Yeah, he kind of does, doesn't he?"

Pixie nodded. "Yes, he does."

Joy punched her friend's inked shoulder. "Thanks for introducing us."

"Oh you're welcome." She jumped up and grabbed her purse. "Well, I'm off to work. Have a great time tonight." She blew Joy a kiss.

Caligula cawed, "Kiss for the birdie, kiss for the birdie."

Pixie laughed and blew him one too. "Stupid, adorable bird." She slammed the door and Joy could hear her laughing as she walked away.

Joy picked up her pencil again and moved to her desk and sat down. She tapped her fingers against the wood, thinking about her father's party. The birthday party was small, just the family and their current significant others. Max was out of rehab, not that that would stop her mother from serving champagne and liquor. It would be a full house. After the fiasco with Lily last night, she knew she couldn't do it alone.

She picked up the phone and called Hawk.

He answered on the first ring and she asked, "How do you feel about going to a party?"

"A party? I thought you hated them."

"I hate people knowing who I am, actually. I don't really hate parties as a rule. But I don't want to go to this one and it's sure to be an exercise in the awful."

He chuckled, the sound rich and warm even over the phone lines. "Well that makes for a great incentive to go."

She grimaced. "I'm sure. It's going to be formal too. It's my dad's birthday."

He hesitated and then spoke, his voice lower and serious, "I see. Are you sure you want me there?"

"I am. One hundred percent. Just remember to stop by and get your rabies shots and passport before we go. You might need both of them."

"I take it we may have to fight our way out of a group of the living dead and flee the country if things go really bad?"

She started laughing. Once she started she couldn't stop. "That about sums it up."

"Should I bring garlic and holy water too?"

"No, but a bottle of wine would be good. I'm taking a gift." She let herself smile and added, "I really liked getting to know your old neighborhood last night. I'd like to say you're going to have fun in mine but the truth is that it's not a lot of fun."

"We'll make our own fun," he said. "What time should I meet you, and where?"

"Um, can you come by here? You know what? If you give me your size, I can get you a suit so you don't have to go all the way home."

Hawk laughed again. "I don't even own a suit, but I can pick one up. No worries. I'll see you at what time?"

"What time do you leave the shop today?"

"I can leave about five; that should give me just enough time to get a suit and head over there. How about seven then?"

"Seven sounds good." She propped her chin up on her hand and let gratitude and happiness wash over her.

"Okay, I'll let you know if anything goes wrong or I'm running late."

"Thanks."

He chuckled again. "I'll let you thank me after I save you from a zombie."

She hung up still laughing. Hawk could always lift her spirits and make her happy. He could make her smile even when she didn't really want to and when things were pretty grim.

CHAPTER 18

Hawk showed up just after seven, carrying a suit over his arm. He rushed into the apartment, his eyes widening at the sight of the delicate blue silk dress and the heels Joy wore. He said, "You look...I don't even know the words for how you look. As you would say, holy hot cakes!" He crossed his arms over his chest and admired the view as she twirled around and then faked a pose for him. "Damn! I wish I had something to draw you with right now."

Her smile grew giant and goofy. "You look awfully good yourself." He did, too. His jeans clung to his long lean legs and hips and his shirt was slightly mussy, as was his hair. She kind of wished she hadn't dressed and done her makeup yet. They could stand to be a few minutes late...

He looked down. "I haven't even put the suit on yet."

"I'm tempted to tell you not to. You're crazy hot just like that."

He gave her a silly grin and she realized he had no response. He was probably thinking about stripping both of them down. She laughed and waved her hand, "But yeah, let's get you into that suit."

Caligula cawed in the corner of the room, "Joy loves Hawk. Joy loves Hawk."

Her mouth dropped open. Her swung around and marched over to the smug bird. "I'm going to kill you."

"Kill you!" Caligula screeched as he hopped around his cage, out of Joy's reach. "Joy loves Hawk, kill you! Pixie's insane."

Hawk stepped for and stared the bird in the eye. "For the record, bird, I love her too."

Caligula eyed him balefully. Hawk gave him the middle finger. Joy collapsed with laughter, her bottom hitting the sofa and her shoulders shaking as she howled laughter.

Hawk leaned over her, a smile on his lips but his eyes series. "Joy, do you love me?"

She looked up at him. Her eyes fastened to his face as the giggles disappeared. She swallowed hard. "I have a confession for the tattooist. Yes, I do. I love you, Hawk Reynolds, ink artist extraordinaire."

He kissed her, letting his tongue slide into her mouth. He tasted of peppermint and warmth. "I love you, Joy Reed. I love you and all your delicious parts." He tipped his head to the side. "Now, did you teach the bird to say it first?"

She swatted him playfully. "No freakin' way! I bet you five bucks Pixie taught that damn thing to say it."

He sat down beside her and took her hand then he drew her into his embrace. "I love you, Joy. You're an amazing woman, and I'd be an idiot not to love you. I don't need a bird to tell me you love me; I feel it, inside of me."

"I love you," she said. She didn't whisper it or stutter. The words came out proudly. She loved him, and she wasn't afraid to love him either. He was the best man she'd ever met, and she knew he was the one who'd helped her to come to the place she was at right then, inside herself. "You've helped me to grow in so many ways and you encourage me. I know I'm not easy. I know I have issues. I know I can be a giant pain in the ass too. But I keep getting stronger and better all the time. You did that, and I love you for it, and for everything you are outside of that."

Hawk's eyes grew bright, the green almost looking emerald. "You're good for me, Joy. You made me really think about what I want, and you push me to be more. You believe in me in ways I don't even know how to explain, but I'm grateful for that, and I'm so glad you came to the shop that day and let me paint you. If you hadn't I might have had to start hanging around with Pixie a lot more often."

Caligula hopped in his cage. "Pixie's insane."

"Yes," Joy said, trying to ignore the bird. "She gets points for playing matchmaker."

"She'd make one hell of a profession out of that."

Joy shook her head. "Don't tell her that, for Pete's sake. She'll try it! Then, besides strays in this apartment, I'll have stray men living her as she tries to find mates for them."

Hawk laughed. "Hell no. I'm not sharing you with anyone." He kissed her fingers and then lightly on her lips. "I'd love to pull that dress up and see what delicious treats are underneath."

She grinned wickedly. "You need to get ready. What's under here is for later."

"Oh, you're gonna kill me with wondering all night." He ran his finger down the cleavage of the dress and smiled when her sigh turned into a slight moan. He stood and headed into the bathroom to shower and change.

Joy sat on the sofa, waiting impatiently for him to come out. When he did, her heart skipped several beats.

The suit clung to his body and accented it. His sandy dark hair had been combed, and his skin gave off an enticing aroma of cologne and soap that drew her in like a moth to a burning flame.

She stood and fanned herself as she walked around him. "Wow. That's really all I can think of to say. Well, that and yummy."

He guffawed. "Yummy?"

She nodded. "Yes, yummy. You look very yummy. That suit is reducing my ability to speak."

"Well, that makes us even then."

"I think we need to play dress-up more often."

He gave her a daring look. "Anytime, baby, anytime."

She laughed when she realized what he meant. "Maybe I need to start shopping online more often." She didn't miss the single eyebrow that raised as she teased him. She picked up the exquisitely wrapped gift she'd laid on the coffee table earlier. "Shall we get this over with?"

He offered her his arm and said, "By all means."

Joy would have liked to simply stay right there and undress him slowly. Or have him make love to her while still wearing the suit. That was a far more appealing idea than heading up to Bel-Air to be with her family. She consoled herself that when it was all over she could bring Hawk back there and let him make love to her for a very long time.

Somehow that made the whole ordeal bearable.

The valets took her keys and she and Hawk strolled to the front door of the magnificent mansion set deep in the high, sweeping grounds of the large estate that Tyler Reed had built, on the grounds of what had once been the estate of a very famous movie star from the 1970s.

The house, 20,000-square-feet of glass, concrete, marble, and vast windows that faced sweeping panoramic views, sat nestled into lushly landscaped trees and grass. Footlights illuminated the walkway and as they stepped up it toward the door Hawk's hand found hers and squeezed reassuringly.

She gave him a smile and then the door opened. The butler, a stuffy and stone-faced man named Riley, inclined his head and said, "Good evening, Ms. Reed."

"Good evening, Riley."

They moved past him and into a stunning grand entrance that featured a massive staircase, shining surfaces and ultra-modern furniture, perfectly faded Persian rugs, and priceless art. Joy didn't even bother glancing at it all; she knew it by heart.

Past the entrance was a wide hallway that led them to one of the living spaces, and to where everyone was gathered. She listened to Hawk's low whistle and smiled when he muttered something about tacky and overdone.

As soon as they walked across the threshold the cameras swept onto them and anger hit Joy hard.

Lily's damn reality show. Of course she'd brought them along.

Joy clenched her teeth and said, fiercely, "You've no right to video me in a private residence without my permission, which you certainly do *not* have. Now remove that camera from my face."

Lily snapped from the other side of the room, "Oh for shit's sake, Joy, just let them do their jobs."

Tyler, seated in a chair and staring down into a glass of whiskey, looked equally uncomfortable for once. "Lily, you cannot force everyone to be on your show. She's stated her position."

Joy's mother, sitting nearby on a plush white sofa, managed a cool smile. Lily pouted.

The camera crew gave each other long looks.

Hawk pulled Joy close as he glared into the cameras. "You don't have my permission either. If I see myself on your show, you'll be not only sued, but you'll be brought up on ethics charges. I know my rights."

Lily groaned and said, "Megan, can you please do something with your daughter?"

Megan gave Tyler a pleading look then looked back at Joy and Hawk. For the first time in Joy's life, her mother looked utterly nonplussed, and Joy felt a small frisson of spiteful satisfaction at the expression.

Tyler rolled his eyes, trying to ignore the fact that there were more women than men in the room. "Megan, could you perhaps take Joy's gift?"

Joy's mother got up. Tonight she wore a long and vivid emerald sheath that set off her figure perfectly. Her hair, the same ash-blond as Joy's, was down and flowing across her back and shoulders. It showed fresh highlights and a good glossing, which gave it the look of extreme health.

She approached gingerly, and Joy handed her the gift. "You look lovely, Mother."

Her mother gave her a smile that didn't quite reach her eyes. "You look... nice as well. I wouldn't have thought that designer made clothes in your size, but how lovely that he does. Every woman should have the opportunity to wear high fashion."

Joy flinched. It should have come as no shock. It was the kind of casual, off-the-cuff thing her mother always said. The hell of it was that her mother had no idea how hurtful her words often were. She was simply speaking honestly. She had no idea that the designer who made Joy's dress made clothes for people who were larger than sample size.

Hawk spoke up, smooth as butter. "Good evening, Mrs. Reed. I see now where Joy gets her looks. It must be a generational thing. I can't wait to see her mother."

Joy blinked. What game was Hawk playing?

Megan turned her head slightly instead of frowning. She never frowned. It was bad for the skin. "I beg your pardon?"

"I just meant if the grandmother and granddaughter are so beautiful, her mother must be too."

Near hysterical laughter bubbled in Joy's chest. She couldn't even breathe for fear she'd release that laughter into the air. It was her mother's turn to flinch, and hard. Joy's eyes went to her father, and to her amazement there was a look of clear amusement on his face.

Megan spoke, her voice dripping ice, "I'm her mother."

Hawk covered his mouth, probably to hide his smile. "Apologies, ma'am. Given the obvious disparity in age, I just assumed...so sorry."

Wow. Hawk could be one catty bastard. He was no softy. Then again, the guy grew up in a rough neighborhood and learned how to do tattoos with oil and wire. He definitely wasn't a softy.

Her mother turned away, two bright spots of color high on her cheekbones.

Tyler stood and walked over, his hand extended. "I recognize you. You were on that tattoo show. Hawk Reynolds, right?"

Hawk nodded. "Happy birthday, Mr. Reed. You've got a fantastic daughter, and a lovely home." He shook Tyler's hand.

Joy stood beside him, her mouth hanging open at how smooth and in control Hawk was. He controlled the room. And damn if that wasn't a turn-on.

Tyler motioned to where he'd been sitting. "Come! Sit down over here and let's talk. I'm fascinated by that tattoo business of yours."

Hawk nodded affably and headed for the sofa nearest Tyler's chair. Joy went with him. They sat and took the glasses of champagne offered by the butler.

Hawk took a sip from the bubbly glass and raised it to Joy and then to her father.

She was astonished by what had just happened. If he hadn't been there, the odds of the cameras being taken out of her face would have been a lot lower, and she couldn't even say for sure whether or not her father would have stuck up for her on the subject either.

He'd managed to neatly foil both her mother and Lily, and the others hadn't even arrived yet. For the first time in her life Joy actually found herself able to relax in her family's presence, though she sensed they were regarding her a great deal more warily than they usually did.

It was like setting a wild leopard loose inside a cage filled with domesticated tigers. Her family was sleek and ferocious, and possessed of teeth and claws designed to wound, but Hawk was lethal.

Her father studied Hawk for a few moments before asking, "So why did you refuse to renew your contract with the reality show?"

Hawk unbuttoned the jacket of his suit and shifted to get more comfortable on the couch. "I didn't care for the intrusion into my life. They began to insist on being part of my personal life as well as being a part of what went on in the shop. That was a boundary I wasn't comfortable crossing."

Lily spoke up. "That's ridiculous. Reality television is just entertainment."

Hawk regarded her with wary eyes. "I choose not to be anyone's entertainment. I don't find that gratifying on any level. In fact, I find it demeaning and self-serving."

Now it was Lily's turn to wear those flags of color in her face. She fiddled with her wineglass and then turned her head to stare resolutely at the nearest wall.

Joy didn't miss the amused look on her father's face. He was pretty much bullied by his kids and wife, something people outside the family would never have guessed at, and while he allowed it Joy had always sensed he didn't particularly care for it much. Maybe he let it go because he felt it was his fault they acted as they did.

He and Hawk chatted for a little longer. Joy sat quietly, just watching Hawk's face. Insecure fears began to form in her mind. Silly ones that started to feel possible after taking him to meet her family. What if he left her? What if they fell out of love as suddenly as they had fallen into it? What if he decided her family was too much to handle?

She squashed the thoughts, forcing them out of her mind as suddenly as they had come in.

There was someone new growing in her skin. Someone who was far less timid and far less insecure, and she wasn't about to let that person she had been rise up and ruin or halt that new person's path.

Her thoughts were interrupted by the arrival of Max. Like his father and sisters, Max was possessed of lightless black hair and slightly swarthy skin. He had gained weight again, he did in every rehab he went to, and he came in with a blonde strapped to one arm.

A stunning, beyond sexy, blonde.

Her low-cut bandage dress was skin-tight and almost see-through. Her chest was enormous, her waist tiny, and her platinum hair hung in beachy, tousled waves around her face. Her collagen-puffed lips were wide and plump and her high heels clicked noisily across the floor.

Tyler Reed stood and walked over to his son. "Max!"

"Hey, Pops. Meet Lorelei."

Lorelei gave them all a picture-perfect white-toothed grin. Her eyes went to Hawk and she squealed out, as she ran over to him. "Hawk! You look so handsome! I saw your show got taken off the air!" The words rushed out fast and high.

Max stiffened as he surveyed Hawk. "You two know each other?"

Lorelei giggled madly. "Oh, why of course. I did this movie where it was all tattoo stuff. Like tattooed bad-ass babes or something, and they called Hawk in to do temporary tattoos on all of us instead of using, like, cheap fake stuff. Well, Morgan didn't need any, 'cause she has lots of real tats, but I don't want any. I mean, my body's my moneymaker and not everyone likes tats on their playgrounds. Imagine me old with silly ink all over this body." She circled particularly around her breasts. Everyone's eyes went to where she pointed.

Joy could only stare. She wasn't the only one.

Tyler asked, "I'm sorry, are you an actress?"

Lorelei promptly sat down and leaned forward so far her breasts threatened to explode right out of the top of her dress. "Of course! Adult actress, for now, but I really want to break into the mainstream. I did some horror films already, you now, straight to DVD stuff, but I know I have enough talent to do more. Not more sex, not that it would be an issue, but more actual acting. Big screen stuff." She smiled at Tyler, almost cooing as she reached out and squeezed his knee. "I hear it's somebody's birthday."

Joy looked at Hawk. He hid a huge grin behind the rim of his champagne glass.

Joy's mother squirmed, her hostility obvious, and across from her Lily sat bolt upright, her face pale and her eyes scanning every inch of Lorelei's admittedly enviable body.

"I see." Tyler cleared his throat.

Lily broke in with a sarcastic laugh. "Well, Max, where did you meet this one?"

Lorelei shot Lily a glare as she appraised Max's sister's body. "In rehab, of course. The same place you met your ex-husband, right? Shame he couldn't stay clean, but everyone knew that was going to happen. Some people are just born to get high."

Joy saw the camera crew look at each other and back at the assemblage. It was obvious they wanted to film this rather extraordinary turn of events but were uncertain as to whether or not they could.

Lorelei spotted the cameras, waved, and said, "Oh, your show's filming! You know you really should maybe think about letting it die. Go out with a bang and all."

Lily snapped, "I assume you know quite a lot about going out with a bang."

Hawk chortled and looked at the floor. Max's face grew red. Lorelei smiled brightly, flashing those toothpaste-white teeth again. "Yes, and that's why should take my advice."

Joy choked on her laughter. Hawk's leg pressed against hers. Stunned silence filled the room.

Tyler, red-faced, stuttered out, "Lily, dear, I think you should dismiss your camera crew for the evening."

Lily, scarlet and obviously at a total loss, did. They departed, and awkward silence suddenly filled the room. Something Joy had never ever noticed before in this family.

She turned to her brother and tried to assess how he was doing. "So what's going to happen now?" The words were before she could stop herself.

He looked at his feet and then back up. "I'm thinking of starting my own production company."

Their father said, "Come again?"

Max shrugged, clearly uncomfortable. "Well sex sells, obviously. But the truth is there's too much porn already out there to really compete with. So I was thinking that since there're so many actresses who have worked so long in the adult industry without ever getting recognition for how good their acting really is..."

Tyler interrupted, "How good their acting really is? Son, are you serious?"

Lorelei jumped up and hurried over to Max's side, right into the middle of the fray. "Yes, we are good actresses. If you have never faked arousal or an orgasm, you have no idea of how hard it is. I mean, it's hard enough when it's just you and the person you're with, but when you have to fool an entire audience, and that can mean millions of people, you'd better be a good actress. And if you think it's hard to fake an orgasm, just ask your wife what it really takes to fake one."

Hawk slid toward the end of the sofa. His laughter was so loud Joy let hers loose too. She knew they shouldn't be laughing. This was deadly serious. Her date, and Max's, had just walked into the hallowed halls of the family home and laid down insults. That wasn't how any of it was supposed to work, and she knew it. Her family was aces at insulting people but they always assumed that they themselves were above being insulted in kind.

Tyler began to laugh, hard enough to shake his entire body. "Touché, young lady. Now tell me more about this production company, Max."

Joy's mother was furious. It only took a brief glance at her face to ascertain that fact, and Joy knew that while she was being silent now that would not be the case later. She felt sorry for her dad; she'd been on the receiving end of her mother's private tirades before and she knew how deadly they could be.

Max shoved his hands into his pockets and grinned at his father. "Most adult actresses make good money but they're limited in what they can do. My idea is to make good, not great, films that let them stretch their acting skills and get out of the industry. The truth is most get into it in order to try to get into mainstream films but find themselves struggling to cross over. Even paying them less than what they would make as an adult actress wouldn't stop them from taking on roles."

"Okay, you've actually got my attention. Go on," Tyler set his empty whiskey glass down.

"I'm thinking direct-to-DVD and streaming films. Not overly long. Not very genre-specific. I was also considering doing a podcast show based around a trio of female bodyguards who get sent out each week on different assignments, sort of like that old television show, but with a steamier, more modern twist."

Joy stared at her brother in surprise, "Damn, Max. You've really thought about this."

He looked sheepish. "Yeah, I have. I mean, I'm never going to be up there with you, Pops, and why try? I've been wasting my film school education trying to get into your shoes, and why do that either? I mean, honestly? I want to make movies, but I don't care about awards and all that, and I don't care if people think I haven't lived up to being your son either if my movies don't win awards. Not anymore. I know what I want to make, and I think I can do it and pull a modest profit. So...so there."

Joy said, "I get it."

Max nodded. "Cool. Thanks, sis."

Tyler leaned back on his heels. His face wore a guarded expression. "Nobody ever expected you to live up to what I did."

Max said, "I'm sure you believe that, Pops."

Calla and Rose arrived with their dates. Joy introduced Hawk. Max introduced Lorelei. The silence became awkward again and then, thankfully, they were all called in for dinner.

Dinner was probably delicious. Joy couldn't taste a single thing. She was seated next to Hawk on one side and Lorelei on the other, and it became very clear very quickly that the rest of her family, with the exception of her father, were doing their best to ignore all of them.

She wanted to laugh about it.

Rose had slept her way around L.A., and Calla was no better. They both drank too much, took recreational drugs, and partied their faces off with anyone willing to supply them with whatever they wanted right then.

Her mother had been the darling of the club-scene in her day, before marrying her dad, who had a long-standing addiction to painkillers that he hadn't kicked until fifteen or so years before.

None of them were any better than anyone else, but they were so self-absorbed and entitled they couldn't see it.

Joy took a deep breath and tried to look at them differently. In a way Hawk might do. Calla had been in a bad car accident several years before. She'd lost her then-fiancé in the crash. Lily had had bad marriages and a heroin habit just as bad. She wanted to be an actress, and instead she was the star of a reality television show. There were people who were famous for nothing more than having multitudes of children, and who were the stars of their own reality shows. Lily couldn't possibly feel like her dreams were coming true, and she was getting older quickly. She was nearing forty.

That jolted Joy to the core. Had all her siblings had dreams that seemed impossible simply because they were the children of people who had already made their dreams come true, and in such a huge way?

It was possible. Her half-siblings' mother was one of the greatest actresses of her time. She'd been terrifyingly beautiful and talented. She'd won every award there was, some twice.

How could any of her children hope to make a name for themselves with that over their heads if they chose to act? And they had all wanted to. Except Max, who'd wanted to make films like his uber-successful father, and herself, and she wanted nothing to do with any part of the industry.

She wanted nothing to do with any of it.

But was she any different than her siblings really? They rebelled and reacted to their lives differently than she had, but she had done rebelled and reacted too. She'd refused to have anything to do with it and she'd struck out on her own to prove she could, and that she was not like them at all.

She remembered Hawk saying he wasn't his family. That he wasn't his neighborhood. But he was at the same time. There were some things he couldn't erase, but he could learn from them and learn all about who he was and wanted to be because of those things, if he just tried.

She understood exactly why he'd taken her to that crumbling and seedy neighborhood and shown her the remnants of his old house.

He had been trying to impress something into her, something she still hadn't seen until just that moment. Her family wasn't the worst on the world, and the people in it were no better or worse than people in most families. They had more money, certainly, but that didn't mean that they weren't scarred from their pasts or from their upbringing.

And like Hawk, and her, and now Max, they could do better if they wanted to.

He was close to his family. He didn't respect his father, but he loved him because he could understand him.

She'd spent her whole life disliking her family because she hadn't been able to understand them. She'd been just as closed and narrow-minded toward them as they had been toward her.

And she'd let herself become exactly what they were.

Insecure.

Unhappy.

It had taken a man who cared for her to make her feel like she had something to offer the world. More than that, it had taken someone able to see past their own ambitions and dreams to see her for who she could be for her to be able to see herself.

Brimming with happiness she'd never really known before, and a self-awareness that was as clear as a bell, Joy let go of all her old animosity toward her family.

It was simple really. She just let go.

CHAPTER 19

Once dinner finished everyone began to leave. Her mother and father were in the kitchen and Joy, on her way in to say goodbye, paused as she heard her mother's voice raised in a heated hiss.

"Of all the nerve. A tattoo artist and a whore! At my table! And while there were cameras rolling too! The sheer..."

Her voice trailed off as Joy stepped into the kitchen. Her father, as usual, stood on one side of the kitchen and her mother on the other, facing off like combatants. He wore the same bland but beaten look he always wore, and Joy found herself wondering again why they even stayed married. She knew why her mother did, actually; she just didn't know why he stayed with her.

She spoke. "You know, Mom, coming from a woman who used to dance topless before she got her big break, and who admitted to sleeping with her photographers to make sure she got better assignments, I find that pretty hypocritical. Maybe you don't like her, okay, cool. But Max does, and she seems to have lit a fire in him nobody else ever has. You should be happy. One less cross to bear."

Her mother's heated face paled instantly.

"Or maybe that's exactly why you don't like it. You're so used to playing the victim in this family. Poor you, dealing with a daughter who's too fat, a stepson who's an addict, and three stepdaughters who have had to deal with so much. You really do enjoy that, I think. That's okay, if that's what you like, but just because you enjoy bemoaning those things doesn't mean that any of us have to remain the cross you like to tote." The words weren't kind, but they needed to be said. Someone had to say them.

Her mother's eyes narrowed. "How dare you—"

"How dare you!" Joy shot back. "It's like you can't stand for anyone to be happy. Dad, me, any of your children. Heaven forbid there's an ounce of happiness in our hearts! You don't let Dad eat anything he likes because of your stupid self-absorption with how you look, and how he looks. Who cares if he puts on a few pounds? He could use them, to be honest, and he's filthy rich. Nobody thinks you married him for love or because you thought him attractive. Not even me. Probably not even him. You might be able to still tell yourself that, but deep down you probably don't believe it either." Now that she had opened the gates, she couldn't stop the flood. "You can't just accept that a kid you had didn't come out looking runway-ready. You can't accept that you never got that big break, and that you were a good model but never a supermodel. You can't get over coming from a dirt-poor family, and so you act rude and stuck up to try to cover up that fact instead of just being grateful and happy that you're here. And that's okay, if that's how you want to live." She threw her hands in the air. "But for shit's sake, stop making everyone around you as unhappy as you are, because that is definitely not okay."

Her mother's lips compressed until they were thin slits in her ashen face. "You have no idea how I feel."

"Yes, I do. People treat other people badly because they feel badly about themselves. That's your issue, not ours. You treat everyone around you like they're beneath you or not able to live up to your ideals. I'm sure that's because that's the way you feel about yourself. I'm sorry for you, Mom, I am. But you don't get to keep doing it. Also, for the record, if you ever call me fat, or big-boned, or make a shitty comment about my size ever again, I'll happily call you on it. It's not acceptable. It was never acceptable. It hurt and it left me scarred and insecure."

Her mother's eyes widened as she shook her head defensively. "I never meant to make you feel that way. I just worry that you aren't healthy, and that whole heart issue..."

Joy crossed her arms and glared. That was her excuse? Really? "It was a birth defect! It wouldn't have mattered if I had been as thin as you. It wasn't from junk food or lack of exercise or anything else. Stop putting insults into neat little phrases like, "I care that you are so unhealthy, not about your weight." Because that's a lie. What you care about is that when I go anywhere with you I don't show up in a size two, and for some reason that embarrasses you on a personal level. You take that as a personal failure. It isn't."

She turned to her father, about to apologize for bursting out like this on his birthday. She opened her mouth, but new, angry words formed. "And what the hell, Daddy? Get out while you still have some life in you yet. Because if it was me, I'd have divorce papers on the kitchen table before the last guest even departed."

He didn't say anything.

Her mother turned to look at him. Her face crumpled. "I don't make you unhappy, Tyler, do I?"

He sighed. "Yes, you do. But that's neither here nor there. I think your daughter is trying to get something through to you, and maybe you should listen."

Her mother shook all over. Her eyes welled with tears. Her lips parted and closed then she said, "How do I make you unhappy?"

Tyler smiled sympathetically, but there was something else there as well. "You're bitter. You're angry. You're cold and unforgiving. You're cruel and judgmental. You're demanding. You give nothing of yourself to anyone, not to me or your child or even the world. But for some reason I still care for you."

Hawk stepped into the kitchen. He spoke gently but firmly. "Joy, I think it's time to go."

Her face colored. How much had he heard? She nodded and took his outstretched hand, and then stopped for a moment to hug her father. "I'm sorry, Daddy. It's your birthday. I shouldn't have said that stuff now and here."

He shrugged. "You never know when or how long you have to say what you need to say."

It was a line from one of his most famous films. On impulse she said, "Do you know what I was thinking about the other day? When I was little, you used to take me with you and the crew to shoot exteriors when you were working on all those films set in South L.A. and you always let me choose which house or street to shoot."

Her father gave her a puzzled look.

She sighed and said, "I think that's what made me want to go into those neighborhoods and better them. Seeing what was there compared to what we had here. In a way, you're responsible for my life's ambitions."

His smile was small but grateful. "I love you, honey."

"I love you too, Dad." She forced a smile in her mother's direction. She seemed a stranger now. "Good night, Mother."

Hawk guided her to the kitchen door and through it. Max stood near the door, a stricken expression on his face. Their siblings were already gone, along with their plus-ones. Lorelei stood near Max, her face neutral. Max said, "Thanks for standing up for me."

Joy shrugged. "I wasn't really. I was standing up for me. You can always claim innocence in that whole thing and run for the hills before it spills over."

They'd never been close, the two of them.

Max said, "Hey, how about the two of you come over to our place in a few days? I'd like to pick your brain about a few exterior shots too. And Lorelei helps with a charity that might be able to help you."

Joy stared at the near-Barbie doll beside her half-brother. "What?"

Lorelei chuckled. "I do a lot of work in the neighborhood you want to revitalize. Your dad told Max about it. You need to get folks onboard, and I know those folks. I could go with you if you wanted to, like, I don't know, sit down and talk to them about it or something."

"Really?" Joy wanted to hug the woman but had a feeling if she did, she might pop Lorelei's large breast and the tiny woman would go flying around the room like a balloon. It was a terrible thought and she tried to push it aside. "That would be great. Like, really. Thank you." Joy's smile was real and warm.

Hawk and Max nodded, and did the guy thing while she and Lorelei stood awkwardly watching. Joy murmured, "I'm sorry my mom said that."

Lorelei shrugged. "I once had a woman refer to me as a mutated ideal of beauty with a set of bolt-on tits and wonky lips. Nothing else has ever come close to that. I think that bar on insults has been lifted way too high."

Joy didn't want to laugh but she couldn't help it. She bent double, laughing, and when she stood up her face was scarlet. "Damn! I wish you'd been around when I was in junior high and high school. You certainly would have put things in perspective."

Lorelei giggled, "Hon, in junior high and high school I was covered in acne, flat-chested, and possessed of one beauty secret. A book over my face. I wouldn't have been of any use at all."

"Really?"

"Really. And so what? That was then and here I am now."

Joy asked, "If you don't mind my asking, what were you doing in rehab?"

Lorelei shrugged. "Rehabbing. I got a little happy with the pain pills. Plastic surgery hurts, you know. Lots of people's lives hurt too. So I wanted it to stop. Seemed reasonable. Same thing with Max. Everyone's trying to staunch the bleeding one way or another, I guess."

"That is remarkably true. I apologize again for judging you before we had a chance to speak." She looked over at Hawk. "I was about ready to tear a strip off of you for flirting with Hawk when you walked in."

"I wasn't—"

"I realize that now. Just a little over protective of that hot stuff over there," Joy giggled.

A low murmur of approval escaped Lorelei's lips. "Mmmhmm, I don't blame you there, girl."

Hawk turned and smiled. "You ready to do?"

"For hours. What took you so long?" she teased as they got their coats from the butler and headed back outside. The air outside seemed fresh and cool, and Joy took in a large lungful of it. As they got into the car she said, "Well at least there weren't zombies."

Hawk turned to look at her, his face twisting with mirth. He grabbed the steering wheel and let loose a torrent of laughter. He laughed until he cried, wiped his eyes, and laughed some more.

"It was that bad, wasn't it?"

He wiped his eyes with one hand and said, "The other day I was wondering how in the hell I was going to take you over to meet my mom and brothers. You're so sweet. So nice. So *normal*. I was worried, really worried, that you'd find us all weird and crazy, and be offended by some of the things that get said. But now—well, I think my family's looking pretty good."

"You want to take me to meet your family?"

"Yeah, but be warned. I've never taken anyone to meet them before, so they'll likely be all over you."

She leaned back in the seat. "I can handle all over. It's the crazy cat fighting my family does that is impossible to live with."

"Then I'd better warn you that in my family the fighting is not nearly as civilized. Forks get used a lot. Don't ever reach for the last piece of bread. My sister, Jenny, she'll stab you with her spoon to get it. No idea why, but she has to have the last piece of bread every single time."

"Well, thanks for the warning." Her smile was wide and she added, "Should I wear boxing gloves?"

"No, they like bare knuckles. They're going to love you especially when they find out about your revitalization project."

She hoped so. She also couldn't wait to meet them. She had feeling that his family was a lot more fun than hers, and a lot less judgmental too.

Or at least she hoped so.

Either way, she was the first woman he had invited home and that said a lot. It said everything.

"Can you take me home now? I really want to fuck you." She smiled sweetly and tried to sound polite as possible.

CHAPTER 20

Joy woke up the next morning to see Hawk's head next to hers on the pillow. There was some stubble on his jaw, giving him a dangerously sexy look that contrasted sharply with the more innocent aspect his face took on while he slept.

She caught herself studying every little line around his eyes and wondering what had made him laugh enough to create them, and at the little strands of hair near the hollows of his temples. The man was simply gorgeous.

Her eyes skimmed lower. The sheets had tangled around his narrow waist, revealing the flat and hard muscles of his abdomen and that feathery little line of hair that led downward, to the part of him she *really* liked, which was nicely outlined by the sheet.

She regarded the thick outline of his cock, and then her hand moved along the sheet, rippling it slightly as she traced the outer sides of his morning erection with her fingers. It stiffened slightly, poking up against the sheet, and a naughty grin lifted her lips as she repeated the caress and watched it swell again.

Hawk spoke up in a sleepy voice. "You do know that if you keep that up you're going to have submit to being ravaged."

"Ravaged?" Her fingers slid below the sheet and skimmed along his flesh, her nails raking lightly. "Did you just say ravaged? What century do you live in?" she teased, her body warming to the image of him ravaging her again, like last night.

"I did." He grinned, his eyes opening in small slits as he looked down at her. "I should've been some historical bodice-ripper. I like the word, and I'm sticking with it."

She let her hand find his flesh; her fingers wrapped around it and his heated skin filled her palm. "I see, but what if I want to ravage you?"

His hips arched slightly as she drew her hand upward, drawing his flesh upward and then moving down again.

She shifted slightly and pushed the sheet down. His organ swelled yet again and she shimmied lower, her head right above his pelvis. "Would you mind if I did this?" She licked and sucked the tip of his head, then lifted her head to see if he'd say no. When his hips pressed against her she grinned and winked at him, then bent her head back to the task. With every lick and suck, he grew stiffer, his hips moving up and down in a slow motion.

His body gave off a sleep-scented smell, musky and masculine all at once. His flesh pulsed and pounded in her mouth and fist. Her body woke and responded as his did, and by the time he tugged her upward, using her hair to do it, she was eager and shaking all over.

She straddled him, her body opening for him as she slid down his hot length and joined them together. Her eyes fluttered close as he pulled her face toward his for a long and searing kiss that sent fresh jolts of desire into her body.

His hand cupped her bottom, his fingers pressing into her flesh. Tomorrow, or even later today, there would be bruises there. His tattoo, on her body.

Her legs shook with desire and her breath came faster as they moved together, sliding toward completion. Her inner thighs pressed him tight and his hands moved upward to her breasts. He lifted his upper body so that he could take her nipples between his teeth and flick his tongue across them. Fresh sensations washed over her and she hurtled toward a climax as his thick flesh parted her inner walls, soaked with her fluids, and then went deeper than before.

She came to her climax and felt him throbbing inside her as he reached his own. She moaned over and over as ripples of pleasure soaked through her and slowly came to a stop. She collapsed on top of him, her sides heaving with exertion.

His arms clasped her body and she let herself roll off him carefully. Her face went to his neck and she nuzzled it as his hand stroked her hair. Hawk grunted. "Damn, woman. You are fine."

She giggled as she snuggled against him. "You're pretty hot yourself."

They laid there together, sweaty and comfortably drunk on love.

Hawk kissed her forehead suddenly. "I don't know if I told you how proud I am of you after last night."

She looked up at him. "You're proud of me?'

"Yes. I am. Why wouldn't I? And it's not just last night."

"I don't know why you would be."

He rubbed her shoulder and then his finger went to the scar between her breasts. "Because you don't try to hide this anymore, or any of your body, when we're in bed. Because you've figured out how to deal with your family. Because you really are going after your dreams. Because you're beautiful and talented and..."

She hushed him with a kiss. The words made her glow but they also embarrassed her. She wasn't used to compliments but she rather thought she could get used to them.

Her kiss was interrupted by the loud clanging from the alarm clock by her bed. Hawk groaned and said, "Damn it. And it's my day to open the shop too."

He rolled out of bed and stretched, his body flexing and twisting.

She watched with real appreciation and then asked, "You free tonight?"

"For you. Always." He dropped a kiss on her forehead. "If I don't get in that shower I'm going to totally miss opening the shop and I've got a high-end client this morning."

"I could join you... in the shower." She was teasing him, but his bare ass and side ab muscles were too distracting.

He groaned. "Don't even tempt me."

Her phone began buzzing so he took it as his cue to disappear into the ensuite bathroom and she heard the water start running. She nodded regretfully, "Yeah duty calls for me too." She'd missed the call on her phone and checked to see who it had been. Her mother.

She was in no rush to return that call. She got up and went to make coffee. When Hawk emerged, fresh and gorgeous, she handed him a cup.

"Anything important on the phone? I was kinda hoping you might join me."

She laughed and shook her head. "I got the impression you need to be at work on time."

"I do." He winked. "But I can always squeeze in a quickie."

She tossed a tea-towel at him. "I'll squeeze you in anytime, babe."

The bird in the living room squawked, "Squeeze you in. Ahhh, I'll squeeze you in."

Joy rolled her eyes. "Figures. Oh, and the phone was just my mother. I'll check it later." The woman was probably going to ream her out for last night.

"Maybe she's seen the light."

"Never." She winked at him. "Now get going before I strip off this t-shirt and make you need to shower again."

Hawk gave her an appreciative once-over. "After work." He leaned in and kissed her neck and then whispered in her ear, "I'm going to make you beg for it." He drank his coffee quickly, then dropped a few more kisses on her mouth before he left.

Joy took her shower and then did her hair and dressed. She was on her way out the door when she checked her phone again. Her mother had tried calling again. Twice.

"Great," she muttered as she slid into her car and dialed her mother's cell number. "Hey, Mom," she said brightly as the Bluetooth kicked in and she pulled out onto the road.

"Joy." There was no happiness in her voice as she spoke.

"I'm on my way to work, Mom. What's up?"

"You don't have to be sharp with me. After the awful night I've had, you could try to be a little kinder."

Joy stared at herself in the rearview mirror. *What the heck?* "Everything ok, Mom?"

"No, it's not! Haven't you heard the news or checked the Internet?"

Joy's gut sank. Something was off. "I haven't had a chance. What's going on?"

"Your father had a massive heart attack last night. They don't think he's going to make it."

"What?" She swerved to miss a parked car as her hands began shaking. "Where is he?"

"At the hospital, of course."

Joy shook her head. "What hospital, Mom? Are you there with him now?"

"Or course not!" she snapped. "I'm home trying to cope. I'll head over later, once the doctors have more news."

"So he's there alone?" Joy began to cry.

"No, there're doctors and staff taking care of him. He's at Cedars-Sinai Medical Center. I let the others know last night."

"What?"

"Are you going deaf, Joy? Really? Must I repeat everything?"

It's called shock. She focused on driving and found herself heading to Hawk's shop. "I'm heading to the hospital. I'll see you there, Mom." She ended the call, not wanting to snap at her mother.

She pulled in front of Hawk's shop and knew she couldn't go inside. She called him instead. "H-Hey. I... I..."

He heard the trembling in her voice. "Where are you? I'm on my way."

"Outside your shop." Tears streamed down her cheeks and she shook so hard she couldn't turn the car off.

He raced outside the shop and swung open her door. Without a word, he reached in and unclipped her seatbelt, pulled her out, and held her in a tight embrace. He stroked her hair and didn't say a word as she sobbed into his shoulder.

"My d-dad. He had a heart attack." More fresh tears spilled down her cheeks.

Hawk nodded and led her around to the passenger side of the car. "Is he okay?" He opened the door and helped her in, clicking her seatbelt back on and rushing around to the driver's side.

"I don't know. My mom said it happened last night. She's not even there!" She buried her head in her hands and used her sleeve to wipe her nose, not caring at all.

"What hospital?"

"Cedars-Sinai."

Hawk eased into the morning traffic and headed for the highway. "Let's go see what's going on."

Joy didn't know how to wrap her mind around what they were going to find out when they got there. She had a terrible feeling they were too late. She swallowed hard. "His heart's been bad for years and...oh, Hawk, why didn't I say something kinder last night?"

Hawk reached for her hand and held it tightly in his. He said, sternly, "You said nothing you have to be ashamed of. You told the truth. That's never wrong. He's older, in his eighties, and he's had a long life. If it's his time, it's his time. You didn't cause this. This is not your fault."

She nodded. She'd put her lustrous hair into a long ponytail and it lay over one shoulder. The sun, streaming through the window, lit her hair up and brought out the golden strands buried deep within it. Her head bowed and she stared down at her hands. They were silent as they drove the rest of the way to the hospital. She let Hawk ask the front registration for her father's room and take her up to the floor he was on. She waited, wringing her hands as Hawk spoke to a nurse at the desk who checked her computer, probably to see who was allowed in to see her father. Finally, she led them into a small office.

A grim-faced doctor came in and before he spoke, Joy knew they were too late.

"I'm Dr. Davoy. I'm sorry—"

"He didn't make it, did he?" she cut him off, suddenly not wanting to know the details.

The doctor's lips pressed into a thin line. "I—no, he didn't. We tried everything. His heart..."

"Was tired," she finished for him.

CHAPTER 21

"I've never lost anyone before. I mean, not like this." Joy sat beside Hawk in another waiting room, this time with her father's lawyers in an upscale part of town. It had been a long two days, a whirlwind of stilted memories. She wore a simple black dress, her hair in a braid. The newspapers and media had been everywhere, and she'd hated it. No. That was a lie. She loved that the papers were painting her father as a wonderful man. They were sad for him. More than most of her family was. "I can't believe he's gone."

Hawk held her hands in his. "I know."

She looked over at him. "Have you ever lost anyone?" She'd never thought to ask him before. It seemed like such an important question now. She wiped the millionth tear that ran down her cheek.

"Yes."

She titled her head. "I'm so sorry I didn't know that. Who was it?"

Hawk's eyes grew bright with moisture. "My oldest brother committed suicide when I was fifteen. He was eighteen."

The words fell into the space between them.

She was silent as she thought about Hawk, just a young man to lose someone so close. She'd had her father for her entire life. Damn, life wasn't fair. "I'm sorry."

"Me too. He was a great guy. His name was Dennis." Hawk's voice held no bitterness. "He was just overwhelmed by life and...he was depressed, had been since early on."

Her brow wrinkled. "Why?"

"He was gay and he hated himself. He thought our parents would disown him if they found out."

She let her fingers go to the date on his arm, surrounded by a heart made of rose thorns and chains. "I see."

She did see; Hawk knew she did. She saw and she understood. "I'm so, so sorry."

Across the room, her mother sat in a chair, her face wearing a shocked and frozen expression, her hair in disarray. She wore a black dress and shoes, but they didn't match. Joy had noticed but hadn't said anything. It didn't matter. The poor woman had lost her husband.

Lily, Calla, and Rose sat on the other side of the room with a woman she recognized. Jennifer Reed. Movie star extraordinaire. She'd been busy working her whole life, and had all but abandoned her children after her divorce from Joy's father.

The woman was almost skeletally thin, but she still radiated a loveliness and presence that caught her eyes and held them. She inclined her chin but didn't speak.

Max sat huddled into a chair; Lorelei sat on the floor near his feet, one reassuring hand on his knee.

Hawk pressed his body against hers and she gave him a grateful smile. Nobody spoke and the silence thickened as did the tension. Hawk kept waiting for Megan, Joy's mother, to decide it was time to hurl harsh words at Joy, and he knew she was waiting for that too, but Megan never said a word until the door opened and a man stepped out.

He introduced himself as George Dapper, Tyler Reed's personal lawyer, and he asked Megan, Joy, and Megan's stepchildren to come into the office. As they were going in, Megan suddenly reached out and closed the door sharply, right in Joy's face.

Hawk, angry and shaken by the cruelty, stood, but before he could do anything, Joy had wrenched the door open and stormed inside.

Jennifer Reed, the rich woman sitting alone on the other side of the room, harrumphed and said, "Well, looks like Megan's in a tiff after all." She stood and stretched, cat-like, and turned to Lorelei, "Do you smoke?"

Lorelei nodded.

"Good." Jennifer grabbed her purse. "I could fucking use one. Let's go outside and have a smoke."

Lorelei stood and smiled, but Hawk saw the warning in it. He hid his grin when Lorelei told Jennifer in a matter-of-fact voice, "Sure thing, but if you're considering taking me out there to warn me away or buy me out of Max's life, you're likely to need them to haul you to the hospital in one of those hearses."

Jennifer's lips quirked upward. "Dually noted. Max sure did pick a fireball, didn't he? Good for him. Besides, why would I do that? I'm sure you pissed Megan off enough at Tyler's party to make your presence tolerable."

Hawk watched them go and then shook his head. Women. *Hollywood women*. He'd never understand them.

He did worry about Joy, though. She was inside a room with a den of vipers. His concern grew as the time passed slowly, and then slowed down even more. He ignored the two women when they came back in from outside and stared at the tattoos on his arm. The lawyer had asked for just the immediate family with good reason. There was enough to argue about in there without adding more people who had no power to make decisions into the mix.

After what felt like an eternity, the family filed out. Joy was pale and shaken, and her hands shook so violently he saw it from across the room. He walked over to her quickly and reached for her hands.

"Can we go?"

He nodded, terrified that someone in that room had hurt her with words that could never be forgiven. He glared at the other females, even though they all seemed too shocked to notice. "Sure, thing," he murmured to Joy and led her outside.

As they drove away, Joy sat silent for a few minutes and Hawk didn't press her. He knew she'd tell him whatever it was when she was ready.

Joy cleared her throat and stared out the window. "My father left an enormous amount of money behind, nearly a hundred million dollars. He left Mom the house and an interest-bearing account holding twenty million, which means she won't be able to blow through it at a high rate of speed." She leaned her head against the headrest. "He's left his older four children five million each. They're all pissed. Each of them. Shocked and ticked off because they found out he left more to charities. Like five million isn't enough money."

"What about you, Joy?" he asked quietly, wondering if the shock on her face was because her father had ignored her.

"He left fifty million dollars in trust. To me." She sighed. "Nobody in that room knew what to say, least of all me. The money's in an irrevocable trust and not for personal gain. It's been hallmarked for my projects in the lower-income neighborhoods." A tremor snuck into her voice. "It's the money I need to finally put my dream into motion. If I wanted to, I could buy the homes, remodel them, and hold the loans for the people who bought them." She let a sob escape as she tried to smile. "He said that my ideas, my project, made him want to leave a better mark ion this world. The lawyer said my father hoped the money would be enough to achieve my dream."

CHAPTER 22

Every day that passed made Joy more grateful for Hawk. He was a solid shoulder and ear for her while they went through the process of burying her father and moving forward.

In the passing weeks, Hawk fended off her half-sisters as they screamed at her, and he dealt decisively with her mother. He also dealt effectively with Max, who'd been angry at first but eventually decided that what was left of his trust and the money he'd gotten from the will was fair enough.

Her mother disowned her.

Joy wasn't surprised, but it was harder than she expected it to be.

She and Hawk lay in bed that night, after her mother's very public announcement that Joy was no longer her daughter and had never really been her kid. She wasn't adopted or anything, it was just like she had somehow come into the world as different from everything her mother had wanted just to spite her.

Hawk's fingers ran over her breasts. "You want to talk about it?"

She wiped her eyes. "What's there to talk about? I knew she would be angry. I just didn't think she'd be this selfish. If my father knew..." her voice trailed off.

"He did it because he believed in what you're trying to do. He didn't stick up for himself much while he was alive so maybe he figured when he was dead there weren't many ways she could fight him. Besides, maybe he also knew that the best thing you could do was sever your ties with her. You were right when you said she's unhappy and toxic. It still isn't fair."

She tried to smile but the tears that never seemed to dry up these days started again. "It sucks."

"It's hard, but maybe he did you a favor. You don't have to run after her either. If she wants to change her mind, she will."

"And if she doesn't?"

Hawk put a hand on her cheek. "Joy, whether you want her in your life or not, she doesn't want to be in it right now, and maybe she never will. Or maybe she will want to, and if she does you're going to have to be strong enough to lay down some ground rules about how she acts. I think your dad knew."

She looked into his face. "How do you do that?"

He smiled. "Do what?"

"Manage to be so right all the time?"

"Not all the time." He winked and then shrugged. "I just learned early in life that people are people. You can't make them into something different than they are. All you can do is give them room to grow."

Joy smiled. "Speaking of growing..."

Six months later, Joy stood next to Hawk, one hand in his at the ground-breaking for the green space in the neighborhood she'd planned to help restore. Hawk let go of her hand and slipped it around her waist.

Overhead, the sky shone a bright blue and she whispered, "Thank you for agreeing to paint the murals on the walls."

He smiled, "Hey, a man's got to do what his gal wants, right?"

"Only if it's what he likes to do," she responded.

His smile was sexy, and slightly hesitant. His fingers went to her arm where, earlier that day, he'd painted a small and beautiful sunrise to mark this day. His smile grew bigger as his other hand slid out of his pocket and he held up a diamond ring. "Think you might want to marry me?"

Her breath caught as she stared at the pretty sparkling ring. "Yes, without a doubt!"

He slipped the ring on and pulled her into a passionate kiss, ignoring the cameras flashing and media pulling their attention away from the ground-breaking to the two of them.

Joy didn't care. She never would've believed that she would fall for a tattooed bad-boy with the sexiest body and kindest eyes she'd ever seen.

Yet she had, and he'd fallen for her too.

He was tattooed forever into her heart.

And she wouldn't have it any other way.

THE END
Surrender of a Tattooist

Find out if Pixie is going to go through another broken heart or will love finally find a way to mend the scars?

Coming March 2016

Surrender of a Tattooist
Book 2

The last thing Pixie wants is another broken heart. She's been through a lot, and she isn't sure she wants to start anything at all with handsome Cliff, one of the best artists in the Flying High Tattoo Shop run by Hawk, who's dating her best friend Katy.

But, as it turns out, Cliff is hard to resist. He's a smartass hottie with a rock hard body and few surprising tricks up his sleeve. Not to mention he has a romantic streak matched only by a determined streak, and he is determined to have Pixie.

But Pixie isn't the only one with a terrible heartache in her past. Cliff's been burned before too and it doesn't take long for those burn scars to start flaring up. Can the two of them find a way to make peace with their pasts in order to have a future together?

Note from the Author:

Thanks for reading Confessions of a Tattooist!

This is one of those series where I fell in with the covers before the story was even created. My amazing cover designer, Kellie, from Book Cover by Design created the first cover and a story immediately formed in my head!

When photographer Dave Kelley shared his image for "Pixie" I knew exactly where the story was headed. It's been so much fun to write this story and wait till you see the rest of the covers! They are gorgeous!

I love to hear from my readers so feel free to get in touch with me. My contact information is on the next page!

If you have a moment, it would be great appreciated if you are able to leave a review on the site you purchased the book on!

I've added an excerpt of my new "Undercover Series'. Hope you enjoy it!

Sincerely, Lexy xx

Find Lexy Timms:

Lexy Timms Newsletter:
http://eepurl.com/9i0vD
Lexy Timms Facebook Page:
https://www.facebook.com/SavingForever
Lexy Timms Website:
http://lexytimms.wix.com/savingforever

Free Excerpt

Perfect For Me
By Lexy Timms
Book 1 of
Undercover Series

Undercover Series

Perfect For Me
Book 1
Perfect for You
Book 2
Perfect for Us
Book 3
Coming March 2016

Description:

They say love comes in all forms.

The city of Pittsburgh keeps its streets safe, partly thanks to Lt. Grady Rivers. The police officer is fiercely intelligent who specializes in undercover operations. It is this set of skills that are sought by New York's finest. Grady is thrown from his hometown onto the New York City underworld in order to stop one of the largest drug rings in the northeast. The NYPD task him with uncovering the identity of the organization's mysterious leader, Dean. It will take all of his cunning to stop this deadly drug lord.

Danger lurks around every corner and comes in many shapes. While undercover, he meets a beauty named Lara. An equally intelligent woman and twice as fearless, she works for a local drug dealer who has ties to the organization. Their sorted pasts have these two become close, and soon they develop feelings for one another. But this is not a "Romeo and Juliet" love story, as the star-crossed lovers fight to survive the deadly streets. Grady treads the thin line between the love he feels for her, and his duties as an officer. Will he get in too deep?

Perfect for Me - Chapter 1

"Thank you, Pittsburgh!" a long-haired rocker screams through the speaker. His voice strains and cracks from his bellowing. "We are Former Legion!"

The cry is answered by a roar of a hundred people jumping up and down for him and the rest of the band. Behind the lead singer, a drummer is elevated on a platform so the crowd can see him. He throws his hands up in the air, crossing his drumsticks in an "X" formation. On either side of the singer, the guitarist and bass guitarist simply bow their heads. Once the crowd returns to silence, the drummer smacks his sticks together, creating a steady beat for his bandmates to play to. He slams down on the pedal to thrum the base drum. Then, he starts smacking the others in the offbeat. The bass player joins in, followed by the guitarist with a chord. Once the music starts, the singer joins in with the words, but his voice is raspy from screaming. The crowd answers with applause and more earsplitting cheers, recognizing the song as a favorite.

The weather is perfect for this afternoon day at the park. Hanging in the sky is the burning July sun. Luckily, a breeze carries mist from the merging three rivers, cooling the crowd along with others spending their day in the park. A grassy field stretches across a peninsula-like land that has rivers on either side, flowing into the third. Far from the concert are regular goers of the park. Some toss a Frisbee while others have brought their dogs for a bit of running, and then there are a few who are lying on beach towels to soak up the rays. Meanwhile, the crowd for the concert hugs the fountain at the edge of the peninsula, spraying cool mist.

At the base of the fountain, a large group has gathered more than to keep cool. While most of them are there for the concert, there are a few that have their attention away from the screaming band up on the stage. One man sits on the ledge of the fountain, completely ignoring the music. He looks to be a college student, judging from his age. Yet, he dresses as if he were homeless. His blue jeans are tattered around the ankles from years of being used. Despite the high temperatures, he wears a red flannel shirt with the sleeves rolled up to give him some relief. A knit cap sits atop a mop of greasy black hair. Sitting on his crooked nose is a pair of thick-framed black glasses. He is scrawny in stature with a thin face. The only thick part of him is the messy beard. While he looks to be unkempt, he is quite popular in the crowd. People come up to him, chatting for a few minutes before walking away and letting the next person approach.

After a young blond strolls away, he is approached by another man a few years older than him. Unlike the toothpick physique of the flannel man, he's lean with thick arms and legs. The flannel-wearing hipster stands up, but is a foot shorter than his new friend, and probably fifty pounds lighter. The muscled man wears an official shirt of *Former Legion* with the band logo splattered on the chest with a mix of dark colors. The short sleeves reveal a plethora of tattoos wrapping his left arm that stop at the wrist. Similar to the hipster, he has a wild mop of hair.

"Can I help you?" the short man in flannel asks, looking at the man with great disgust.

"You Andy?" the tall man asks.

"Maybe, who wants to know?"

"The name's Grady," he answers. "I've a friend who says you know where I can find some good *Italian*." He stares Andy up and down. "What do you say?"

The hipster, Andy, looks up at this man with a suspiciously raised brow, but he lets his backpack slip off his shoulder. "Yeah, I got what you're looking for."

He unzips the pack. Grady looks inside to find it filled with small plastic bags. Each of the sandwich-size bags is stuffed with brown mushrooms that look as thin and scrawny as the hipster that has them. They are long stemmed with a brown cap and some look to be dried out. The guy with the rocker shirt reaches for one, but Andy smacks his hand away.

"You got to pay first, dude," Andy scoffs, pushing the glasses back up his nose.

"How much is a bag?" Grady asks.

"Small bag is twenty, big bag is fifty."

"Small bag then." Grady goes into the back of his cargo shorts for his wallet. Without opening it up, he slips out a crisp Andrew Jackson and slaps it in the hipster's hand.

After putting the twenty in his pocket, Andy looks to his customer. "I didn't quite catch the name of your friend who told you about me."

Grady smiles. "My buddy Mario."

"Oh, you know Mario," Andy gives a smile back, "hold on, this stuff you don't want. Anybody that Mario recommends gets the good stuff."

Zipping up the bag of mushrooms, Andy opens a pocket on the side of his backpack. Grady waits patiently with his arms folded while the hipster fumbles through the pack. A scream on stage catches his attention, turning to see the lead singer down on his knees, howling into the microphone. When he looks back to the hipster, he is met with an unpleasant surprise. Two silver prongs bury in his stomach as Andy presses the button on the Taser. It sends fifty thousand volts of electricity through him, turning Grady into a ragdoll. He falls to his hands and knees as the jolt seizes his muscles. He tries to fight the numbing effect, but the constant current has him sprawling on the ground a few seconds later, twitching slightly. As he lays there stunned, his ocean blue eyes turn to Andy, who crouches beside him. He feels something on the back of his head, a hand no doubt. Andy is petting him like a dog.

The hipster gives a snarky smile. "Tell Mario his princess is in another castle, you fucking nark."

Pretending that nothing happened, the drug dealer, Andy, walks off. His backpack is closed and flung back over his shoulder. With the concert still blasting music, everyone around them is deaf to Grady's groans. The numbing effects of the stun gun start to wear off, letting him twitch a bit more. Shakily he regains control over his arms. He pulls himself up on the seat of the fountain as he gets a tingling in his legs. Forcing his body to stand only causes him to stumble backwards and nearly fall in the fountain. Thankfully he gets enough motor skills back to catch himself from making a big splash. He tries again and this time is able to stand upright. He tries to take a step, but it's wobbly. Like a newborn, he stagger-steps his way after the drug dealer. Andy is oblivious to the pursuit, the footsteps drowned out by a guitar solo. Taking a few more steps has Grady gaining better control over his legs. From wobbly-leg to walking to a light jog. As he gets closer, his large stature casts a shadow over the unsuspecting drug dealer. Andy notices and turns around.

"Shit!" Andy curses under his breath when he sees the cop after him.

The hipster turns around and takes off running. Grady forces his slightly numbed muscles to go after him. Every step strengthens the control over his legs, allowing him to power through the tingling sensation in both legs. His longer stride helps close the gap between them. Andy looks back to see that the policeman is gaining on him. Both men leave the peninsula, heading toward downtown Pittsburgh. Separating them from the rest of the city is an underpass with a waterway and a small bridge crossing over it. Andy runs toward the bridge, but grabs on the railing as he gets to the end. Using his momentum, he vaults himself ten feet through the air, landing in the grass on the other side of the underpass. From there he goes into a dead sprint toward the rising skyscrapers. Behind him, Grady makes use of his longer legs to keep pace, but not tire himself out. Only open space separates the pursuit, giving Grady a small window before the fugitive is lost in a jungle of cars and tall buildings.

The hipster is able to stay out of reach long enough to make it to the street. He expertly weaves in between the moving traffic. A car slams on its brakes as the driver spies the flannel-wearing man running carelessly through the moving cars. Andy does not break stride, but he leaps over the hood of the car as if he were a frog. By the time Grady even reaches the edge of the road, the drug dealer has landed on the other side and is sprinting down the sidewalk.

"Fucking parkour hipsters," Grady complains as he runs headlong into traffic.

Although he's fast, he does not have the same finesse as the man he is pursuing. He runs around the slower cars, but the faster vehicles impede his path. He makes an attempt to push through, but it only causes tires to screech and horns to blare. Grady reaches into his pocket, grabbing his wallet again. Thrusting it into the air, he shows the angry driver the golden shield of the Pittsburgh Police Department. Immediately the honking ceases. It allows him to navigate through traffic a touch easier.

By the time he emerges on the other side of the street, the image of Andy is shrinking. He's about fifty yards away. Sighing to himself, Grady runs after the hipster again. Once more, the longer legs give him an edge. The undercover cop is able to close the gap to about twenty feet before the hipster tries to duck behind a building. A large gap separates the two skyscrapers, which has been transformed into a pleasant park-like area. While it is appealing to the sight, it gives the drug dealer no coverage.

Andy realizes he cannot hope to hide so he runs again.

Grady charges like an angry bull while the hipster does an unnecessary no-handed flip over a park bench. Ignoring the fire in his lungs, the cop gives one final push and throws himself around the ankles of his target. Both men fall to the ground, but

Andy does not throw his hands up to take the impact of the fall. He hits the gravel face first. Blood stains the rocks as his nose and bottom lip bleed. Grady gets to his knees and puts his knee on Andy's back.

"You are—"

An unexpected elbow to the throat has Grady falling on the ground and Andy back on his feet. He runs out the other end of the park, seeing a flow of people on the streets. Bruised and bloodied, he screams, "Help, help, somebody help me!"

Once the blood is seen, a crowd forms around the drug dealer. One man wearing a baseball jersey approaches, "Are you all right, what happened?"

Playing innocent, Andy points an accusing finger. "That man did it. He's crazy, you got to help me."

The crowd suddenly is forced open, as Grady pushes through the people after the hipster. Andy screams again. All of a sudden, Grady feels his arms being pulled behind his back. Two men have snatched him and are pulling him away from the hipster. He tries to shout at them, but his words are muffled by a sudden punch to his jaw. Some cheer for the heroic bystanders. Everyone is caught up in the action that they fail to see a flannel-wearing drug dealer slip away. Meanwhile, Grady struggles to break free of the three men that are trying to hold him down. He is forced to kick one to wrench his arm free. Grabbing the other man, he throws him over his shoulder. The guy falls harmlessly into the bushes. Before the third guy tackles him, Grady pulls out his badge.

"I'm a cop," he pants, showing his shield to everyone in the angry mob. When he notices Andy is not among them, he asks, "Did anyone see where that guy in the knit cap went?"

"The one in the flannel?" an old lady walking on the street overhears him. "Yeah, I saw him heading toward Clemente Bridge."

"Thank you," he says. Just before he runs, he turns back to the two men that are still on the ground groaning. "Sorry for being rough."

The crowd parts like the sea for Grady to pass through. He runs at top speed for the Allegheny River. It does not take him long to spot the unmistakable flannel shirt and wool cap of the hipster, Andy. He runs harder. Behind him, he hears the deep drone of a bus horn as it swerves from hitting him. A taxi makes a sudden stop in the middle of his path, forcing Grady to hop and slide across the hood of the car. The cabby pops his head out of the driver side to shout, but the cop is too far away to hear. Both men weave in and out of the remaining traffic as the bridge comes up on them.

The yellow bridge arcs over the river, with dozens of people walking across it to get to the baseball stadium on the other side. Grady pushes his way through the crowds only to find Andy standing at the center of the bridge. The drug dealer is near the edge with his backpack in his hand. He looks to the river below. With a firm grip on the handle of his pack, he starts to swing it over the railing.

"Freeze," Grady barks.

The command startles the hipster, making him hesitate. He looks over his shoulder. Grady is about twenty feet away with his gun drawn. The crowds of people walking toward PNC Park turn the other way and run for the roads. The bridge empties out as the two men standoff.

"What're you going to do, shoot me?" Andy laughs.

"Just give me the backpack and I won't be tempted to. You've pissed me off enough today."

Pushing on his thick-framed glasses, Andy laughs, "This is the only thing you got to incriminate me on. Once I drop this, your whole case against me goes bye-bye."

Grady watches the backpack hang over the side of the bridge, but a smile comes to his face. "Once I bring you in on drug charges, it won't be hard to get a warrant from a judge. When we search your house, I bet there'll be tons of those little spores, won't there?"

The smug smile fades from Andy as he pulls the backpack onto the bridge. Grady steps closer, lowering his gun as he takes a pair of handcuffs out of his back pocket. When he gets close, Andy surprises him by throwing the pack in his face. In the confusion, the drug dealer grabs the gun. Grady is left with the pack in his hands while the hipster has the weapon. The snarky smile returns to his lips as he points the barrel directly at Grady's chest.

Instead of panicking, Grady taunts him, "You aren't going to shoot me. You're just another two-bit drug dealer. You're not going to become a cop-killer now."

"Shut up," Andy loses his cool. The hand that holds the gun trembles. "You don't know me, you stupid cop."

Andy proves him wrong by squeezing the trigger. It does not budge. The safety had been on the entire time. Grady rushes him. With no more options available, Andy thinks of the only means of escape. Reaching for the ledge, he throws himself over the railing of Clemente Bridge.

"No, don't," Grady shouts as he lunges for the hipsters' blue jeans.

Unexpectedly, the weight of the drug dealer is enough to pull Grady over the railing along with him. Before both men go into the river, he grabs the steel edge, feeling Andy's weight in the other hand. The hipster is dangling by his jeans over the water. He starts to panic, flailing as if it will pull him back to safety. The sudden jerking motions loosen the poor grip Grady has already. He feels them slip an inch closer to the river.

"Stop it, or I'll lose..."

It is too late to warn Andy any further, as he loses his grip and both men go falling toward the river. Grady thinks fast and keeps his body rigid and straight on his way down. He stays surprisingly calm as the water comes quickly up to greet him. The hipster on the other hand is still in a blind frenzy of fear. He flails his arms wildly half-expecting to sprout wings and fly. All the way down, he screams at the top of his lungs. Grady is the first to hit the water, slicing through it like a knife. His body plunges a hundred feet below the surface. Darkness swallows him up along with the water. Luckily he keeps himself from losing orientation. With only a lungful of air, he starts his ascent back to the surface.

The black still has him in its grasp after a couple seconds of swimming, but soon a small flicker of light from the surface peeks through the veil. Higher he climbs, ignoring the aching feeling in his chest. He does not stop. The light seems to stay far away, but it gets brighter. Air in his lungs is all used up and his body begs for more. His head becomes hazy. It shrinks his thoughts. Only *swim faster* runs through his mind. Muscles start to scream at him, aching for oxygen. His lungs are heavy, hurting, burning. Unable to keep holding it any longer, he exhales ten feet below.

Now airless, he struggles to swim faster. He tries not to inhale again, though his body strains for him to take a breath. Higher he swims, five feet to go. Every inch seems torturous, mocking him. The surface gets closer, but the pain grows. Unable to stop himself, he takes a deep breath. Fresh air fills his lungs and the rest of his body. The haze around his head lifts as he survives. He takes another breath, and then another, sucking in air like it is a shot of his favorite whiskey. Relief comes over him as he bobs steadily up and down along the waves of the Allegheny River. But then, he feels something solid bump against the back of his head. Turning around, he finds a body floating next to him in the water.

Andy lays face-first in the water. Blood seeps into the blue, his body shattered upon impact. Unlike Grady, the hipster hit the water sprawled out, unable to punch through the surface. It was the same as if he hit concrete.

Grady curses under his breath, but then he pushes the body into the water. "You're a complete asshole, you know that. Rot in hell!"

The corpse sinks into the depths as it fills with water. Unable to do much else, Grady is forced to swim back to shore. With his strength nearly drained, he is dragged along with the current. It takes quite a bit of effort to get close enough to shore. He finds himself along the bank, and pulls himself out of the water. The first thing he does is kiss the concrete like a long lost lover, ignoring the temperature singeing his lips. Ignoring the clothes clinging to his back, he rolls over and lies on the shore for a moment. He never felt so happy to be back on dry land. Even as the muscles in his arms and legs throb in pain, he smiles.

The heat coming from the sun starts to hurt, forcing him to get up. Every joint in his body aches when he moves, but he tries his best to ignore the pain. Stepping onto the grass buys him some relief. As he is walking, he spots a man standing by the now emptied stage holding a silver square. On a closer look, he recognizes it as a flask.

"What do you have there?" Grady asks, showing the man his badge.

"Uh, I," the man slurs. The stench of alcohol seems to ooze from his pores. "I-It's nothing."

"I'm not going to arrest you," Grady sighs, "just tell me what it is."

The man looks a bit confused at the soaking wet police officer. Still, he answers, "Jack, officer."

"Good." Grady snatches the flask out of the man's hands. He tilts his head back and drinks deep until there is nothing left. The burning sensation running down his chest brings a small numbing sensation to his body. It will help him deal with the pain for now. Pushing the flask back into the drunkard's hands, Grady waves him off. "Thanks for the drink."

Perfect for Me - Chapter 2

In the heart of downtown Pittsburgh, Grady steps out of a taxicab, still dripping water from his river plunge. The cabby is none too pleased with him, but doesn't complain when Grady hands the guy an extra twenty dollars for the fare. The taxi drives away, heading in the direction of the setting sun. Grady walks through the front door of his precinct, each footstep sloshing. He leaves a trail of shoe-sized puddles behind him. When he steps onto the tiled floor, a tennis shoe lets out a shrill squeak.

The receptionist hears the cry and looks up from her computer. She sees a sopping wet police officer standing on the other side of her desk. Water drips off the tips of his bangs. It slithers to the bridge of his nose then to the tip of his chin. He looks at her with a smile, but it causes her to shrink away. She can sense the foul mood that he is in. "Lieutenant Rivers, *literally*." She looks him up and down. "Rough day?"

"You've no idea, Lenore." Grady sighs. "I'm bloody soaked, sore, and wiped. I just want to fill out the paperwork for the case, get out of these wet clothes, and then probably pass out in my car." He goes to the door and stops. After fumbling through his pockets he turns to her. "Could you let me through?"

"Don't you have your ID?" She raises her eyebrows and frowns. This isn't the first time.

"Probably at the bottom of the river by now." He shoots her a look. "Or it could be in the belly of some fish, swimming back up the Monongahela. Can you please let me go through?" he says through gritted teeth.

Lenore rises from her desk. The little receptionist waddles over to the door and slips a keycard through the slot. The light on the electronic lock changes color from red to green. Grady pulls the door open and walks into the precinct. His shoes seem to squeak louder than they did at the entrance. Slightly annoyed by the sound, he pulls his wet shoes off and decides to walk the rest of the way in his soaked socks. He makes his way around a corner, which leads to a long hallway. Walking at double speed, he bursts through the double doors at the end of the corridor. On the other side is a room filled with desks. They are spaced out evenly, creating a grid of four by four in the room. The gap between them is enough for one person to squeeze through at any time. Grady walks three desks in and two deep.

A small plaque has the name "Lt. Grady Rivers" etched in fine gold upon a black surface. The wet lieutenant reaches into his second drawer. He pulls it open almost until it comes off the track. Pushing aside a few papers and oddities, he tosses a grey t-shirt that has the Pittsburgh Police Department insignia inked on the back. Against his cold and pruned fingers the cloth seems warm to the touch.

"Did you take a dip today, lieutenant?" He hears someone laughing at him.

Grady turns to see that he has an audience. In the back of the room, three officers gather around a desk. Two of the policemen stand on either side of the third who sits in his chair with his legs propped up on the top of his desk. The man in the chair is the one who threw the joke, while the two men laugh like obedient lackeys.

Grady looks at the jokester, finding him sneering like he usually does. It shows off his crooked teeth, yellowed from smoking for fifteen years. His expression always looks as if it is scrunched, with a long nose and a whisker-like mustache sitting on his upper lip. A "weasel face" is the best description Grady ever had for the man. Of course, he never said it to the guy's face. Even in his sour mood, Grady cannot help but imagine seeing an actual weasel in a uniform. He resists the temptation to laugh as he turns back to his desk.

Slamming the drawer shut, Grady tries to ignore their laughing as he pulls off the soaked shirt. Wringing it out sends river water cascading to the ground in a torrent. A puddle already forming, sloshes at his feet. In disgust, he tosses the shirt to the floor. It makes a sloppy suction sound as it hits the tile. He reaches for the dry shirt when he hears catcalling and whistling coming from the three idiots behind him. Of course, it's all to mock him. Ignoring them to the best of his ability, he gets dressed.

"Aww, no sneak peek at the panties, Grady?" the weasel-faced man laughs. "Are you saving yourself for Mario when you see him next?"

Dry shirt on, Grady looks at the man with wide eyes. "Rick, what did you just say?"

The guy sneers, "I just happened to hear that Mario was in the neighborhood and needed some mushrooms." When he sees the fury in Grady's eyes, Rick laughs harder. "Holy shit, you actually said it. You actually said the informant was Mario. Hah, you got to be some special kind of moron to believe me. What happened? What did—?"

Rick does not get the chance to finish his sentence as something flies at his head. He does not have time to dodge, as a black box smashes against his face. It knocks him off his chair, sending him flat on his back. Crawling to his feet, Rick knocks the smashed pieces of the telephone off his chest. One of his lackey officers helps him get to his feet.

"What the hell?" Rick demands.

Grady has climbed over his own desk and leaps for Rick. The weasel-faced officer tries to stop him, but he's weaker than Grady. Both men are sent to the ground, with Rick pinned to the floor. He screams as a strong hand wraps itself around his scrawny throat. A fist collides with his face, and then another.

Grady continues his onslaught, punching him relentlessly. Even as his knuckles start to break and bleed, he does not stop. "You son of a bitch," Grady seethes.

Rick cries, "Get him off of me."

One of the lackeys comes up beside Grady and punches him in the temple. It knocks him off Rick, who scurries away, black and blue and smothered in blood. Cowering behind his desk, he watches Grady fight off both of his men. The young lieutenant is able to overpower the two, sending one flying into a chair. One of the lackeys gets up and throws a coffee mug at Grady, but it misses wide right. Instead, it hits the head of another officer who had chosen to stay out of the fight. The glass shatters against the man's temple, cold coffee spilling down the side of his head along with a bit of blood. He turns to the culprit, looking more enraged than harmed. Standing up, the officer is by far the biggest man in the precinct.

He trudges over to the lackey who threw the mug and heaves a punch. Unfortunately, it misses and strikes another officer. It creates a domino effect. Chaos spreads across the entire precinct, as it erupts into a brawl. Brothers in blue fight one another to make them black and blue. Fists are flying in every direction. Even Grady gets hit by a few wild fists. He decides to return them, knocking the policemen flat on their backs. In the midst of the scrap, he notices Rick trying to crawl his way out of the fight. Leaping over a desk, Grady throws all his weight onto the weasel-faced man. Both on the ground, Grady continues to pummel, but Rick gets in a few good hits this time. He lands one on an already bruised cheek, causing Grady to wince. Yet rather than back off it only makes him madder. Wrapping his hands together, he brings both fists down on Rick like a hammer. The blow hits him in the temple.

Somehow over the uproar of the fighting, a door opens with a low screech. All at once the fighting dies. The combaters stop, turning their eyes to a man stepping out of an adjacent room.

He's a tall, but slender figure with wire-framed glasses sitting perfectly on the bridge of an almost perfectly round nose. Under the white florescent lights his bald cranium glints with an oiled sheen as if it were freshly polished. Nothing about the lanky man seems foreboding, but his ice blue eyes make the men freeze. Like frightened children, the officers of the precinct scramble to get back to their desks and sit still as if nothing had happened. Every one of them sits perfectly still, like a group of sentry statues.

"What the hell's going on?" he demands, looking about the precinct for someone to speak up. No one does. Then he finds Grady still pinning Rick to the ground. They are the only two that have not returned to their desks. "Richard! Grady!"

When they hear their names called, both men jump to attention. "Yes sir!"

"Just what the hell are you two doing?" he shouts.

Rick wipes the blood trickling off his lower lip before pointing a finger. "Grady started it."

"I'm sorry to say, but it's true," Grady answers. "I let my anger get the better of me when Officer Mather gave me false information on my case. It jeopardized the undercover sting."

"Don't be so dramatic, Rivers," Rick sneers. "It was just a joke."

Grady shoots him a seething glare. "Well, your *joke* blew my cover. The drug dealer's dead, because of it."

"It's not my problem you're such a shitty cop."

"You son of a bitch." Grady turns to throw another punch.

"Both of you, in my office," the chief barks loud enough to make both men flinch. "Now!"

Like a pair of students being called down to the principal's office, Rick and Grady walk single file to his office. The Chief of Police is the last to enter, slamming the door shut behind him. His two officers stand on one side of the desk while he takes a seat on the other. On the front is a plaque similar to Grady's, but it reads "Chief Robert McArthur".

Robert sits there for a moment, letting the bitter rage simmer from him. A vein on his bald head throbs as he allows the two policemen to stew in fear. "Now, let me get this straight," his eyes send a chill down their spines as he talks in a deep baritone, "you gave him false information on an undercover sting...as a joke?"

Grady can see sweat starting to roll down the side of Rick's face.

"Well, yeah, but I told him the mushroom dealer was named Mario. Like the video game character. Come on, Grady, how did you not get that I was joking?"

"Because I trusted you," Grady snarls. "You said it was direct word from the chief. Thanks to you and your dumb-ass joke, I was nearly killed!"

"You're being dramatic again."

"The drug dealer pulled a gun on me! I wrestled it off of him, but then he made an attempt to jump off Clemente Bridge. When I tried to grab him, I went over too. We both fell. I lived, he didn't." Grady turns to the chief, "You might want to get ready about the media, because there were a lot of bystanders."

The chief turns to Rick. His face has turned a shade of red and the vein has bulged out of his temple. "Rick, I put you on desk duty hoping it would stop you from screwing around while on the job. It seems to me that it only gave you enough time to come up with something *really* stupid. So, you want to crack jokes while wearing the badge? Then go and find another department. You're out of mine."

"Fired?" Rick says, stunned.

"Did I stutter?" McArthur says with a tongue as sharp as a knife. "Get your personal belongings out of your desk by the end of your shift. Now, get out of my sight." Rick angrily looks over at Grady as he steps out of the office.

Grady turns to follow.

"Not you, Grady, we are not done talking," McArthur spits out.

Too tired to fight back, he submits to the command, closing the door behind Rick. Not one ounce of remorse in his body for the dickhead who just lost his job. "Sir, I understand I messed up today by letting the perp get the upper hand. I'll accept any punishment you have in store." He straightens his arms and flexes them, trying to warm his chilled body. He expects the worst. McArthur isn't a guy to let anyone get away with anything.

Instead, the chief takes off his glasses to rub the bridge of his nose. He sighs and asks, "Grady, how long have you worked at this department?"

Grady has to think for a moment. "About eight years. I joined the academy right as I finished college. You were the one who suggested that, remember?" He grimaces. McArthur doesn't need to be reminded of things. The guy knows everything.

"Yes, yes, I remember." McArthur leans back in his cushioned seat, making the springs creak. "You graduated top of your class at the academy, an energetic cadet full of vim and vigor. In eight years you have jumped up to lieutenant. You're a good cop, Grady, a damn good cop."

"Thank you sir," he says with a hint of pride in the smile he cannot hide.

"If I had five of you I would never have to hire another jackass like Rick again," he shouts, loud enough so the entire precinct can hear him. Then he drops his voice to almost a whisper, "Incidentally, there are other parts of the country that are in need of men like you."

"Wait, am I being transferred?" The color drains from his face. "All due respect, sir, but I'd rather stay in Pittsburgh. I've put eight years of my life into protecting this city. Hell, I grew up here. I can't just leave a place I've put so much time and energy into."

"Relax, kid, no need for the dramatic speech." The chief grins. "No, you're not being transferred. I'm just loaning you to the boys up north."

"How far north?" He raises an eyebrow, still not impressed.

Chief McArthur crosses his arms as he smiles. "It's the big leagues for you, kid. It's New York-fucking-New York. That's how far north. A city so nice they named it twice."

Grady rolls his eyes to the ceiling before quickly making his face unreadable. "Why would they need a guy like me?" He had an idea. He didn't mind taking risks. His buddies in high school always called him fearless. Crazy-stupid more than fearless, but still... He knew he had smarts and courage. He should have been a Navy SEAL, but protecting the home front at home seemed more important to him.

"They need an unfamiliar face for an undercover operation, that's why." The chief grabs a manila envelope on his desk and opens it. He spills its contents out.

Grady watches as the chief sorts through the papers. He separates them into three neat piles. The stack on the left side of his desk has some files, from what Grady can see. It's information about a rampant spree of drug dealings occurring throughout the Big Apple. The lieutenant looks to the middle pile, finding information about a case relating to the drug dealings connecting to a specific dealer. On the right is a picture instead of documents. It's an image of an older gentleman judging from the wrinkles on the side of his face. Otherwise, it's too blurry and the man is covered in shadows to make out anything else distinct.

"The NYPD has been trying to take down one of the biggest drug rings in the city for years. They've had little success," the chief explains as he looks over the papers. "The organization has seen some arrests, but they've all been the lowest men on the totem pole, if you catch my drift. The NYPD has tried to hit the syndicate at every angle in hopes to stop them, but nothing sticks. Somehow the group stays one step ahead. Now they want to try and wriggle a guy into the group and take it down from the inside. "

"And you want me, even after my blunder?" Grady hears the words slip out from his mouth before he can stop them. The NYPD must've tried going undercover before, just either not had success or lost a cop.

"I can overlook that," Chief McArthur says. "You won't be working with any amateurs on this undercover sting. They want to bring this group down."

"Got it."

"Good. I already sent your information up to NYPD. They took a look at your file and agree you'll be perfect for the undercover op. Given the way you look and your tattoos, you'll blend right in with the scum of New York."

Grady shoots his chief a harsh look, ready to chew the man out. Instead, he just chews on the corner of his lower lip. "Yeah, good thing I look like a criminal."

"I mean no offense, Grady." The chief senses the rage brewing in the bowels of his lieutenant. "Besides your outward appearance, the fact that you have no living relatives will make it hard for the drug ring to find out who you really are. Plus, you've been working drugs here for two years. You know your stuff. Truth be told, you're the best man for this kind of job. They hand selected you."

"Got it," Grady says as he looks down at the papers. "What do they want me to do while I am undercover?" He knew NYPD would fill him in there, but they'd have set something up prior to fill McArthur in.

"They already have an informant to get you inside," Robert explains. "He can get you in contact with a drug dealer who often works with the syndicate. It'll be up to you to work your way in, of course. Once you get in with the syndicate, you'll have to gather as much information about them so the NYPD has a case against 'em. That means you can't let your cover get blown until the case wraps up."

Grady got it. The group would get too cautious to allow a foul up like a mole happen twice. Dead once. Call me stupid. And dead. "How long will I be gone?"

"That'll be up to you, kid." The chief grins. "Get in and out quick and you'll be home to enjoy some of my wife's turkey. Or maybe the next turkey dinner. It's all a matter of how well it works out. You know."

Grady did. "When do I leave?"

"Here are the tickets for the plane to get you there. It leaves at seven on Thursday. Gives you enough time to pack. Rest up before you go, kid. And come back." He handed Grady the tickets and stuffs the papers back in the envelope before handing that to him as well. He leaves the photo. "I'd come to see you off, but I'm going to have my hands full being down two officers."

"Yeah, I got it. Thanks for the sentiment anyways." Grady starts for the door, when his attention turns back to the shady picture on the desk. "Chief, you never said anything about the guy in the picture."

Robert McArthur looks at the picture for a moment. He rubs his grizzled chin, squinting his eyes as he tries to remember. "Oh yeah, NYPD believe he's the head of the drug op. It's the best picture they have. As you can see it's of poor quality. Not much is known about the frontrunner, except he goes by the name Dean."

Grady stares at the picture curiously. "Why's this picture the only one we could get?"

"It's the only pic that Dean has ever sent to the department," Chief McArthur says, his tone darkening as he hands Grady the photo. "It came in a package sent directly to the NYPD. Along with the picture was the head of the man who took it."

Perfect for Me - Chapter 3

Twilight settles in the downtown area of Pittsburgh with the stars beginning to take their shapes in the blackened sky. Grady gazes out the window of his apartment, watching the moon rise over the horizon. Retreating from the glass, he finds comfort in the one bedroom living quarters. The décor is set to the classic lifestyle of a typical bachelor. In the sink dishes are piled high in an unorthodox fashion. One wrong move and the tower will end up collapsing. Some of them still have traces of dinner from three days ago.

In the living room and bedroom, clothes lay strewn across the carpet. Most of the beige rug is hidden under laundry. Stepping over them, he takes a seat at the kitchen table, which he has converted into a desk. Beside the placemat is a stack of old case files. Tapping his finger against the wood, he thinks for a moment, only to rise again and head into the bathroom, which is probably the cleanest place in his apartment. A white sheen glosses the tiled floor. Grady steps over to the sink, and is greeted by a reflective version of him in the mirror. Ocean blue eyes stare back at him, a man with shaggy blond hair and a scruffy beard.

"No more rugged ass road look." He laughs at himself, as he reaches for a spot on the sink.

Beside his toothbrush is his electric razor. It's already plugged into the outlet beside the sink, so he hits the button. The razor makes a slight humming sound, vibrating gingerly in his hand. Carefully, he takes the jagged edge up to his head and runs it across the mop. Strands of hair fall into the sink. The razor mows a perfect line down the middle of his head, leaving either side high. Grady chuckles at the bizarre haircut before continuing.

Each pass over his scalp removes more from his head. All of it floats into the sink until it looks like a furry creature sleeping in his bathroom sink. A few trims here and there, he shuts the razor off and rubs his head. The crew cut feels stiff to the touch, but it's much cooler than the long locks he had moments ago. He brushes away a few loose strands still clinging to the top of his head and shoulders. Once he's satisfied, he turns the razor to give himself a closer shave.

"Not bad, not bad at all," he thinks aloud. Taking the hair in the sink, he scoops it out of the bowl and tosses it into the waste bin sitting on the floor. He jumps in the shower, washes hair and dirt off his body, carefully rubbing over the bruises from the episode earlier. They might not be showing on his skin yet, but he can feel the soreness already pushing through. Turning the water off, he grabs a towel and rubs his face and head to remove any follicles still hiding, along with the excess water.

Exiting the bathroom, he hears a familiar tune coming from the kitchen. Picking up his pace, he finds his cellphone singing the song *Bad Boys* by a stack of papers. Before the ringing ends, he grabs the phone and places it up to his ear. "Hello?"

"Is this Lt. Grady Rivers?" a gravelly voice asks.

"Who's calling?" Grady asks suspiciously. While he sounds pleasant on the phone, he walks into the living room to grab his gun.

"This is Commissioner Baxton, NYPD," the man answers. "I understand you're the man who'll be working with us."

"I am," Grady says. Stepping to the window, he peeks from around the corner. Outside of his apartment there's a black vehicle parked along the street. "Why're you calling me now?"

"Well, the day of your assignment's been moved," the commissioner says. "We need you in New York ASAP. I've sent a car. It's outside waiting for you."

Bull shit. "Oh, that's kind of you," Grady says, taking the safety off of his gun. "And how do I know you are who you say you are?"

"Cautious man, I like that," Baxton says with a guffaw. "The car may not be an official NYPD vehicle, but the man driving it is."

As if on cue, the driver side door opens. A tall, yet slightly stout man steps out onto the curb. Even from the second floor, Grady sees the large silvery mustache crawling across his upper lip. He's also able to see the cellphone placed up to the man's ear. The commissioner hangs up the phone and waves to Grady up in his apartment. Deciding to play along, the lieutenant slips away from the window and goes to the front door. He tucks the gun in the back of his pants, pulling his shirt over top of it. Going out of his apartment, he takes the grimy steps, his footsteps echoing against the metal stairs. At the bottom he stands in the foyer, only to see the mustachioed man is still standing there. Grady steps out of the building to meet with the so-called commissioner.

"You're probably wondering why the commissioner of the NYPD is meeting with you personally."

"Yeah the thought crossed my mind." Grady holds his hands behind his back, his fingers itching to touch the steel behind him.

The man gives an earnest smile. "Well, this case is very important to me. It may sound a bit cliché, but you're my last hope to catch Dean."

"Pretty words, but like you said over the phone, I'm a cautious man," Grady says, taking a step closer. "How do I know you are who you say?"

"I guess I could make a quick call to clear this up," the man says, as he dials a few numbers on his phone. He places it to his ear and waits. After a minute, the commissioner turns his back and listens carefully to the other person. Grady grabs the gun tucked under his shirt, but does not draw it. He listens carefully to the conversation. "Yes, how are you this evening? Yes, I'm good too, thanks for asking. Anyways, I'm in your neck of the woods. Yeah, sorry I didn't tell you. Our undercover operation took a bit of an unexpected turn so we'll need him sooner. I know. I know. I'm standing here with Grady, but the boy refuses to move. He's a cautious one, just like you said. Do you think you could speak with him? Okay, thanks."

The supposed commissioner hands Grady the phone. Taking it carefully, he brings it up to his ear with one hand while the other stays with the gun. "Who is this?"

"A tired man," he hears the voice of Chief McArthur on the other end. "The man you're talking to is indeed Commissioner James Baxton. You can trust him."

"Understood, sir." Grady is about to hang up.

"Wait, Grady," the chief stops him.

"Yes sir?"

"Good luck."

"Thanks." Grady ends the call and tosses the phone back to the commissioner. "Well, I guess I'm your man."

A smile creeps under the silver mustache. "All right then, lieutenant. Grab your stuff and let's go."

"Yes sir." Grady runs upstairs, empties his garbage and already near-empty fridge. He stuffs a bag full of clothes and toiletries, and locks his apartment. Wrapping his door with a final knock, he chews the inside of his cheek. *I'm coming back*, he assures the door.

Grady steps outside and climbs in on the passenger side of the black car. Before he can even fasten his seatbelt, the engine roars and the tires spin wildly. The black Mercedes speeds off into the night. A few short turns has them across a bridge heading toward the highway. With the window down, Grady can see the moon casting its eerie white glow onto the water. The waters of the Monongahela ripple, distorting the lights. It looks like white ghosts glancing upon the river.

"You're thinking this may be the last time you'll see it," Baxton says aloud.

"What? No I wasn't—"

"Don't try to deny it, kid. It's plain to see you have deep roots in this city."

Grady takes one more look out the window. The city's illuminated with hundreds of lights coming from the towering skyscrapers. Seeing it in all of its beauty brings a smile to his face. "It may be the last time, you never know."

"Listen, kid," the commissioner speaks frankly, "I've no intention of shipping you back here in a pinewood box. You have my word you'll see your city again."

"Wow, thank you." Grady is somewhat touched by his words, but also tries not to sound sarcastic. He's about to go undercover to catch a drug king nobody can touch. Undercover. Holy shit. What the hell is he doing?

"Yeah, well, enough of this sentimental talk." The commissioner's face turns serious. "We have six hours before we get to New York. That'll give us time to go over your assignment and your identity while undercover."

Grady takes one last look as the city shrinks in the distance.

Baxton clears his throat and plays with the thermostat of the car. "Now, how much did Robert tell you about the case?"

Grady slumps in his seat in order to get comfortable for the long ride ahead. "The chief gave me the basic rundown. I'm going undercover to work for an average run-of-the-mill drug dealer in order to work my way into the good graces of the syndicate, which is the real target."

"Partially true," the commissioner says, hitting the accelerator as they travel through tunnels. "Your real target is Dean. He's the brains to this whole thing. Bring him down and the rest will crumble." The lights of the tunnel cast them in an orange glow. The Mercedes drives up behind a tractor-trailer truck, only to pass it once they emerge on the other side. "I'm sure your chief told you, but we have an informant to get you in with the drug dealer. After that it'll be up to you to get close to Dean." The car accelerates again once they are on the highway. "Look under your chair. There's an envelope that contains your new identity."

While the black sports car weaves in between slower cars, Grady feels for the envelope under his seat. It takes a few tries, but he eventually finds the manila envelope. Breaking the adhesive seal, he spills the papers into his hand. A driver's license is paper clipped to the top of the documents. Taking it in his hand, he studies it closely. The picture they used to make the fake identification is one from his actual driver's license. Like now, his hair in the picture is trimmed with a crew cut, although it has a more militaristic styling to it. Similarly, all of his physical features are identical to his actual driver's license. That is when he realizes it is a Pennsylvanian license. The only difference is that it says he is from Philadelphia instead of Pittsburgh.

"Wait, shouldn't I be from New York?" Grady flips the card over and sees it's a perfect fake.

"The fact you're from Pennsylvania instead of New York makes little difference," Baxton says, as they pull up to a toll booth. "Our informant goes by the name Tony Miller. You'll be playing the role as his cousin who has come to New York to find work in order to pay off your gambling debt."

"Got it." He looks back at the license. "So I'm going by the name Grady Miller. I'm Tony's cousin from Philly who needs to make some quick cash to get loan sharks off my back."

"Yes," the commissioner says. "You also will be suffering from a gambling addiction. That's what got you in this predicament. You'll be meeting with a sponsor of Gambler's Anonymous in New York. That's how you'll keep in connection with us."

"Clever," he admits.

Baxton turns to him. "Now, I suggest you rest up before we arrive in New York City."

Grady shrugs. "Sir, I don't mind staying awake."

"You don't understand, Grady. Our informant has told us the drug dealer is expecting you tonight at three. That's the reason why I came to get you early."

Grady feels a slight tingle running along the length of his spine. He ignores the sensation. This is his job. He'll do whatever he needs to keep people safe.

As nerve-wracking as the undercover work sounds, he manages to shut his eyes and fall into a light sleep. While he has his eyes closed, he can feel every twist and turn the car makes. An unexpected swerve jars him awake for a few seconds, but he falls back asleep shortly after. While he lies there sound asleep, he cannot help but remember the trips he used to take with his father. He would often sleep in the car while his dad drove. The nostalgic notion makes him uncomfortable. Sitting up in the car, he forces himself awake.

His head is swimming from the abrupt way he woke up. He doesn't want to think about his father. Or anything family related.

As if on cue Baxton says, "We're here."

Looking out the window, Grady sees they've come to a stop by a street corner. Under the street lamp is a young man who appears to be around the same age as Grady. He's wearing a baseball cap with the brim tilted to cast a shadow over his face. Despite it being hot and dry, he wears a black long sleeved shirt. The cargo shorts and backpack completes the typical apparel Grady sees on criminals roaming the streets this time of night. Grady gets out of the car, but not before tossing his gun in the passenger seat. The commissioner only nods before driving off into the city. The undercover officer is left alone in the foreign city with a mysterious man in black.

Walking up to the guy, Grady asks, "You Tony?"

The shadowy figure steps forward and wraps his arms around Grady. "Hey, Cuz! How you doing? Good to see you, man! How's Aunt Shelly been?"

Grady's confused at first before realizing Tony's already playing the part, so he plays along too. "She's been good. Not too happy about me playing the ponies, but you know." He shrugs, trying to remember how much cash he's got in his wallet and that he left his bag in Baxton's car.

"I hear yah," Tony says. "Come on, I want you to meet the guy."

The two of them start walking down the block, reminiscing about a childhood that does not exist. Both of them laugh, taking to the role almost instantly. Tony makes a sudden right at the end of the street, forcing Grady to trail behind him. The informant strolls down another block, and then makes a left. Grady follows. Another half a block, Tony stops outside an Italian restaurant. Grady takes a look at it. The place looks like a dive. A neon sign that spells out "ITALIA RISTORANTE" in cursive hangs overhead. Some of the letters are missing while others are just blacked out.

Grady follows Tony inside, taking a mental note of the bullet holes through the front door.

Much like the cover of a book, Grady was too quick to judge. The inside of the restaurant is lavish. Its space is large enough to fit well over fifty people comfortably. Round dining tables are covered in white linen. Each has a candelabrum sitting in the center. Well past closing, the candles are out for the night, except for one. In the corner there is a single customer taking in a late night snack. A man sits in one of the three booths against the wall. Three candles are lit so he can see what he is eating. On his plate is enough spaghetti to fill the stomachs of four people. Yet the guy does not seem to slow down, as his fork stabs at a meatball the size of Grady's fist.

He watches as this portly man shovels the entire thing in his mouth. The customer is an older guy with a balding head covered by a greasy comb over. Sweat causes the glow of the flames to glisten on his face. His cheeks are round and puffy like a baby's.

Double chins are somewhat concealed behind a long goatee, which is also caked in tomato sauce.

Grady and Tony approach him as he slurps up a spaghetti noodle. He looks up from his plate as sauce splatters on the bib tucked into his jacket. Two brown eyes shift from one guest to the other. They stop at Grady. "Who's this guy?" he asks, he points at the unfamiliar Grady with his fork.

"This is my cousin Grady," Tony, the informant answers, smacking his *cousin* firmly on the back. "He came here all the way from Philly for work. Needs some help paying off some gambling debts."

"That true?" the greasy man asks, taking another forkful of noodles into his mouth.

Grady lies, "Yeah, I play the ponies. Don't have any luck, as of late."

"Fair enough," he turns his fork from Grady to Tony, "I want you to take your cousin out and pick up a package for me. It's an easy job. If he can pull it off, I'll consider him." He stares down his nose at Grady. "You may look like a tough guy, but that don't mean shit in this line of business. You got to have the balls for this work. Let's see if you got 'em." He slides a slip of paper across the table.

Grady picks it up and reads it. Written on it in sloppy handwriting is an address. Committing it to memory, he crumples the piece of paper and tosses it back on the table. Giving the stout man a nod, he and Tony walk out of the restaurant. Once they are out in the open air, he turns to the informant. "We passed the address on our way here." Grady turns down the street they came on and starts walking.

Tony runs ahead of him to block his path. "Wait a minute, Cuz, how do you know this is the right way?"

"I recognized the street name from our little stroll." Grady points down the road to a green street sign hanging from a traffic light. "The address is 147 Mott Street. That sign over there says Mott Street."

"Impressive. I always took you for an idiot," Tony says and laughs. "Now come on, this is going to be an easy job." Together they walk down the street to the intersection. Even in the dead of night, the traffic lights operate as they do in the day. Across the street is a glowing orange hand, but Grady ignores it. Halfway across the street, he looks back, waiting for Tony to cross. The informant runs after him, "So, what do you—"

"Quiet down," Grady wraps his arm around the guy and pulls him close, "we're being followed."

Tony and Grady hold their collective breaths, listening. It's faint, but a steady stream of wheezing comes about twenty yards back towards the restaurant. Managing to stay inconspicuous, Grady takes another glance over his shoulder. A plump and round shadow stops. It clumsily dives into an alleyway, waddling as fast as the pair of stubby legs can.

"My guess, that's the dealer keeping an eye on us." Grady nods in the sneak's direction.

Tony agrees, "Yeah, Miles likes to keep a careful watch over the new recruits."

"Miles," Grady snickers. "The guy looks like he hasn't walked a mile his entire life."

"Ha, good one man!" Tony chuckles. "Just don't let the boss hear it. Oh yeah, Miles likes to be addressed as 'boss', so keep that in mind too."

"Will do," Grady answers, making more mental notes. He looks up at each of the stoops that they pass along the street. Each of the residential mailboxes has their house numbers plastered on the steel in white lettering. The houses seem nearly identical, with minute changes made by the homeowners to make them somewhat unique. His ocean blue eyes read the numbers one by one. On the fourth house, they find it.

Tony's the one who hops up to the door, pounding his fist.

From the other side of the door, they hear a woman shout in a raspy voice, "It's in the mailbox!"

Tony checks the mailbox. His hand reappears with a square package the size of a CD case. Brown deli paper wraps the contents to keep them safe. The informant waves to Grady with the package in hand and bounces to the street. As his feet touch the pavement, red and blue lights start flashing. They grow brighter as a vehicle draws closer. Grady's body tenses when he sees the familiar glow flash against the face of the house.

"No, no, not now," Grady growls under his breath. When he turns around, he sees a patrol car parked a few feet away with two policemen stepping out. Their guns are drawn.

Across the street, Grady is able to catch the swollen sight of Miles trying to hide behind a shrub. The red and blue lights flash across his swollen face. He seems to be studying Grady, watching to see what he'll do. With little to no option, the undercover cop does the only thing he can think of. "Book it," he shouts to his cousin.

He takes off running down the street with Tony trailing behind him. The officers chase after the pair of criminals. Being in better shape, Grady gets farther ahead, creating space between him and the cops. When he hears the footsteps growing fainter in his ear, he glances back over his shoulder. Tony is trying to keep up, but he's red in the face, gasping for air. Similarly, the cops also appear to be tiring. He decides to use it as an opportunity. Once an alley comes up on his right, he runs to it and ducks behind the brick wall. There, he waits.

Footsteps grow louder as someone approaches, but he knows they belong to Tony. When the informant comes into view, he grabs the guy by the collar and drags him into the alleyway. "When the cops come, I'll tackle the one and you can get the other. Knock him out as quickly as you can."

"No wait," Tony objects to the plan. "These guys are in on this, it's all staged. We wanted to make a good first impression so Miles would trust you."

"What?" Grady shakes his head. "Why didn't you tell me?"

"I thought you knew," Tony says while he rests against the wall. He's still struggling to catch his breath.

Grady turns his attention back to the street just as the two police officers come panting into the alley. One is doubled over, holding his knees while he gasps for air. The other presses his back against the wall, using the brick for support.

"Holy shit," the older looking of the two says between breaths. "Are all you Pittsburgh cops that fast?"

"Yeah, every single one of them," Grady lies.

"You're nuts," the younger one remarks.

"Thanks, and thanks for the help." Grady wants to knock the two guys out. Who has time for chit-chat?

"Anything to catch Dean," the older cop says. "By the way, I'm Dan and the rookie over there is Casey. If you ever need help in the big city, we can help you out."

"Okay." Grady looks at both their faces, hoping their images will stick to memory.

Dan glanced back to the streets. "I don't see Miles, but you two better hide so it looks like we lost you."

Suddenly, Grady gets an idea. "That fat lard'll take a while to catch up to us, unless he's got someone else working with him. Let's make it a bit more believable."

"What do you mean?" Tony asks.

Grady points to the rookie. "Casey, punch me."

"What?"

"Punch me," he repeats himself. "Hit me in the eye. It'll make things more believable."

"But...I never hit anyone before."

"It's true," Dan chimes in. "The poor rookie has yet to see any action in the field."

Grady smiles. "Come on, rookie, give me your best shot." *Stupid dumb-ass.*

The rookie walks up to Grady, who stands easily six inches taller. The young officer trembles, his arms look like straws when compared to the muscular, seasoned officer. Still, Casey obeys and curls his right hand into a fist. Still trembling, he winds back. He tries to focus on Grady's right eye. The rookie swings, but closes his eyes at the last second. Knuckles connect though not where Grady had hoped. The fist strikes.

"Ow, you mother fucker," Grady curses, his hands reaching for his nose. He bites back a cry of pain.

His fingers feel his entire nose is bent toward the right side of his face. Blood pours out of his distorted nostrils like a red waterfall. It stains his face and hits the ground, creating a crimson puddle at his feet. Overcome with pain and rage, Grady merely reacts. He throws a punch of his own. Unlike the rookie, he hits Casey square in the eye. The blow sends the rookie flying off his feet. He comes down with a loud thud, crashing hard on his back. He does not move, he does not get back up.

Grady looks over when he hears a grunt coming off to the side. Tony's standing over the other officer. The older cop is lying flat on his stomach, knocked out cold like the rookie. Grady's about to speak when he catches the sound of heavy wheezing coming from the street. Whirling around, he sees Miles standing a few feet away.

Sweat's falling from his face in a torrent, staining the collar of his shirt and underarms. He's huffing and puffing like a fairy tale wolf. It takes him a moment to gain his composure. "That...was...amazing," he says between his panting. "You're so strong, man, so fierce...it's fantastic! You're a good man, Grady, a very good man. Perfect and fearless. Much better than you," he points to Tony. "He's exactly what I need in my group. Strong. Fast. Not stupid. And you can stay out of trouble." Miles continues to pant. He wipes his forehead with the bib still around his neck.

"Thank you sir—I mean, boss." Grady makes the slip, but Miles does not notice. He holds his hand up and then readjusts his broken nose. It hurts like hell, but it's happened before so Grady braces for the pain, and then the release of pressure.

"Yes, come back to the restaurant," he says, managing to stand upright. "I have a place upstairs. We need to celebrate."

The three conscious men leave the alleyway, making their way back to the restaurant. Miles leads them through the kitchen to a flight of stairs in the back. At the top there is another door. He opens it, allowing Grady and Tony to enter his apartment. It is just as large as Grady's back in Pittsburgh, but not quite as luxurious. The couch in the corner appears to be as old as New York City itself. Grady can see a few springs poking through the cushions. Beneath their feet the carpet is old and decrepit with some patches of rug missing. Wallpaper is peeling. Still, it is a roof over their heads.

"You boys can stay the night if you like," Miles says as he tosses Grady a towel. "What do you drink?"

"Anything. I need one," Grady says, still feeling the throbbing pain in his nose. Tony just nods.

"Good, good." Miles waddles to the arch leading into the kitchen. "Lara, baby. Get three beers in here. Now!"

Grady steps out of the way to allow Lara entrance into the living room. The woman walks in with three cold ones in her hands. She stands a head over Miles without heels on. Her hair is long blond locks that hang down to her shoulders in waves. She has skin the color of cream and as smooth looking as silk. She's beyond gorgeous. Not rough, fat or ugly like Miles. She's wearing a friggin' tight black dress that shows every curve and muscle on her sexy body. Dang, she didn't belong here!

Deep pools of hazel stare only at Grady. He meets her gaze and cannot help but gape back, unable to tear his eyes away.

End of Excerpt
Perfect for Me
Is FREE

More by Lexy Timms:

Book One is FREE!

**Sometimes the heart needs a different kind of saving...
find out if Charity Thompson will find a way of saving forever
in this hospital setting Best-Selling Romance by Lexy Timms**

Charity Thompson wants to save the world, one hospital at a
time. Instead of finishing med school to become a doctor, she
chooses a different path and raises money for hospitals – new
wings, equipment, whatever they need. Except there is one
hospital she would be happy to never set foot in again—her
fathers. So of course he hires her to create a gala for his sixty-fifth
birthday. Charity can't say no. Now she is working in the one
place she doesn't want to be. Except she's attracted to Dr. Elijah
Bennet, the handsome playboy chief.

Will she ever prove to her father that's she's more than a med
school dropout? Or will her attraction to Elijah keep her from
repairing the one thing she desperately wants to fix?

** This is NOT Erotica. It's Romance and a love story. **

* This is Part 1 of an Eight book Romance Series. It does end
on a cliff-hanger*

Managing the Bosses Series
The Boss
Book 1 IS FREE!

Jamie Connors has given up on finding a man. Despite being smart, pretty, and just slightly overweight, she's a magnet for the kind of guys that don't stay around.

Her sister's wedding is at the foreground of the family's attention. Jamie would be find with it if her sister wasn't pressuring her to lose weight so she'll fit in the maid of honor dress, her mother would get off her case and her ex-boyfriend wasn't about to become her brother-in-law.

Determined to step out on her own, she accepts a PA position from billionaire Alex Reid. The job includes an apartment on his property and gets her out of living in her parent's basement.

Jamie has to balance her life and somehow figure out how to manage her billionaire boss, without falling in love with him.

Hades' Spawn MC Series
One You Can't Forget
Book 1 is FREE

Emily Rose Dougherty is a good Catholic girl from mythical Walkerville, CT. She had somehow managed to get herself into a heap trouble with the law, all because an ex-boyfriend has decided to make things difficult.

Luke "Spade" Wade owns a Motorcycle repair shop and is the Road Captian for Hades' Spawn MC. He's shocked when he reads in the paper that his old high school flame has been arrested. She's always been the one he couldn't forget.

Will destiny let them find each other again? Or what happens in the past, best left for the history books?

The Recruiting Trip

Aspiring college athlete Aileen Nessa is finding the recruiting process beyond daunting. Being ranked #10 in the world for the 100m hurdles at the age of eighteen is not a fluke, even though she believes that one race, where everything clinked magically together, might be. American universities don't seem to think so. Letters are pouring in from all over the country.

As she faces the challenge of differentiating between a college's genuine commitment to her or just empty promises from talent-seeking coaches, Aileen heads to the University of Gatica, a Division One school, on a recruiting trip. Her best friend dares who to go just to see the cute guys on the school's brochure.

The university's athletic program boasts one of the top hurdlers in the country. Tyler Jensen is the school's NCAA champion in the hurdles and Jim Thorpe recipient for top defensive back in football. His incredible blue-green eyes, confident smile and rock hard six pack abs mess with Aileen's concentration.

His offer to take her under his wing, should she choose to come to Gatica, is a temping proposition that has her wondering if she might be with an angel or making a deal with the devil himself.

Seeking Justice
Book 1 – is FREE

Rachel Evans has the life most people could only dream of: the promise of an amazing job, good looks, and a life of luxury. The problem is, she hates it. She tries desperately to avoid getting sucked into the family business and hides her wealth and name from her friends. She's seen her brother trapped in that life, and doesn't want it. When her father dies in a plane crash, she reluctantly steps in to become the vice president of her family's company, Syco Pharmaceuticals.

Detective Adrien Deluca and his partner have been called in to look at the crash. While Adrien immediately suspects not everything about the case is what it seems, he has trouble convincing his partner. However, soon into the investigation, they uncover a web of deceit which proves the crash was no accident, and evidence points toward a shadowy group of people. Now the detective needs find the proof.

To what lengths will Deluca go to get it?

Fortune Riders MC Series
NOW AVAILABLE!

Undercover Series - Book 1, PERFECT FOR ME, is FREE!

The city of Pittsburgh keeps its streets safe, partly thanks to Lt. Grady Rivers. The police officer is fiercely intelligent who specializes in undercover operations. It is this set of skills that are sought by New York's finest. Grady is thrown from his hometown onto the New York City underworld in order to stop one of the largest drug rings in the northeast. The NYPD task him with uncovering the identity of the organization's mysterious leader, Dean. It will take all of his cunning to stop this deadly drug lord.

Danger lurks around every corner and comes in many shapes. While undercover, he meets a beauty named Lara. An equally intelligent woman and twice as fearless, she works for a local drug dealer who has ties to the organization. Their sorted pasts have these two become close, and soon they develop feelings for one another. But this is not a "Romeo and Juliet" love story, as the star-crossed lovers fight to survive the deadly streets. Grady treads the thin line between the love he feels for her, and his duties as an officer.

Will he get in too deep?

Heart of the Battle Series
Celtic Viking
In a world plagued with darkness, she would be his salvation.

No one gave Erik a choice as to whether he would fight or not. Duty to the crown belonged to him, his father's legacy remaining beyond the grave.

Taken by the beauty of the countryside surrounding her, Linzi would do anything to protect her father's land. Britain is under attack and Scotland is next. At a time she should be focused on suitors, the men of her country have gone to war and she's left to stand alone.

Love will become available, but will passion at the touch of the enemy unravel her strong hold first?

Fall in love with this Historical Celtic Viking Romance.

* There are 3 books in this series. Book 1 will end on a cliff hanger.

*Note: this is NOT erotica. It is a romance and a love story.

Knox Township, August 1863.

Little Love Affair, Book 1 in the Southern Romance series, by bestselling author Lexy Timms

Sentiments are running high following the battle of Gettysburg, and although the draft has not yet come to Knox, "Bloody Knox" will claim lives the next year as citizens attempt to avoid the Union draft. Clara's brother Solomon is missing, and Clara has been left to manage the family's farm, caring for her mother and her younger sister, Cecelia.

Meanwhile, wounded at the battle of Monterey Pass but still able to escape Union forces, Jasper and his friend Horace are lost and starving. Jasper wants to find his way back to the Confederacy, but feels honor-bound to bring Horace back to his family, though the man seems reluctant.

NOTE: This is romance series, book 1 of 3. All your questions will not be answered in the first book.

Coming Soon:

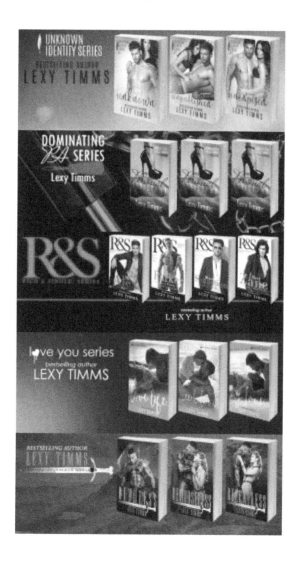

Don't miss out!

Click the button below and you can sign up to receive emails whenever Lexy Timms publishes a new book. There's no charge and no obligation.

Did you love *Confession of a Tattooist*? Then you should read *Unpublished* by Lexy Timms!

Bestselling romance author, Lexy Timms, brings you a new series that'll steal your heart and take your breath away.

Unpublished - book 2 of the Unknown Identity Series

Things with Colton didn't go as Leslie has planned and after running back to New York City, she's the most surprised person in the world to find him standing on her doorstep, asking for a chance to win her heart over.

Leslie doesn't know how to respond. But, Colton's here, alive and wanting to love her.

Excited to show her new found beau the city she's come to love, Leslie realizes when Amber and Jsoie return, that she left out one minor detail about her life.

The more Colton expresses his love for her, the more Leslie grows nervous about telling him who she really is.

Will Colton being willing to accept who she really is when the truth comes out?

Also by Lexy Timms

Alpha Bad Boy Motorcycle Club Triology
Alpha Biker

Fortune Riders MC Series
Billionaire Ransom
Billionaire Misery

Hades' Spawn Motorcycle Club
One You Can't Forget
One That Got Away
One That Came Back
One You Never Leave

Heart of the Battle Series
Celtic Viking
Celtic Rune
Celtic Mann

Justice Series
Seeking Justice
Finding Justice

Managing the Bosses Series
The Boss
The Boss Too
Who's the Boss Now
Love the Boss
I Do the Boss
Gift for the Boss - Novella 3.5

Saving Forever
Saving Forever - Part 1
Saving Forever - Part 2
Saving Forever - Part 3
Saving Forever - Part 4
Saving Forever - Part 5
Saving Forever - Part 6
Saving Forever Part 7

Southern Romance Series
Little Love Affair
Siege of the Heart
Freedom Forever
Soldier's Fortune

Tattoo Series
Confession of a Tattooist

Tennessee Romance
Whisky Lullaby

The University of Gatica Series
The Recruiting Trip
Faster
Higher
Stronger

Undercover Series
Perfect For Me
Perfect For You

Unknown Identity Series
Unknown
Unpublished
Unexposed

Standalone
Wash
Loving Charity
Summer Lovin'
Christmas Magic: A Romance Anthology
Love & College
Billionaire Heart
First Love
Frisky and Fun Romance Box Collection
Sexy Bastards Anthology

Made in the USA
Coppell, TX
28 July 2024

35274550R00134